EXACT FARE ONLY

EXACT FARE ONLY

*GOOD, BAD AND UGLY RIDES
ON PUBLIC TRANSIT*

EDITED BY

GRANT BUDAY

ANVIL PRESS • VANCOUVER

Exact Fare Only Copyright © 2000 the authors

All rights reserved. No part of this book may be reproduced by any means without the prior written permission of the publisher, with the exception of brief passages in reviews. Any request for photocopying or other reprographic copying of any part of this book must be directed in writing to the Canadian Copyright Licensing Agency (CANCOPY) One Yonge Street, Suite 1900, Toronto, Ontario, Canada, M5E 1E5.

CANADIAN CATALOGUING IN PUBLICATION DATA

Main entry under title:

Exact fare only

ISBN 1-895636-29-9

1. Local transit—Anecdotes. 2. Commuting—Anecdotes. I. Buday, Grant, 1956-
HE4211.E92 2000   388.4   C00-910953-6

Cover: Rayola Graphic Design
Photos by Mandelbrot
Printed and bound in Canada

Represented in Canada by the Literary Press Group
Distributed by General Distribution Services

The publisher gratefully acknowledges the financial assistance of the B.C. Arts Council, the Canada Council for the Arts, and the Book Publishing Industry Development Program (BPIDP) for their support of our publishing program.

Anvil Press
Suite 204-A 175 East Broadway,
Vancouver, B.C. V5T 1W2
CANADA

CONTENTS

Introduction / 9

REFLECTIONS

Bussing It by Jean Mallinson / 15

Diary of a Mad Bus Driver by Brian Pratt / 25

The Doors on the Bus Go Open and Shut: True Funnies by Eve Corbel / 31

Where It Hurts by Betsy Trumpener / 37

The Fare by Tim Hearsey / 39

The Customer Is (Eventually) Always Right at B.C. Transit by Bob Smith / 43

Heat by Stephen Osborne / 47

TRAVELLING

Pilgrim Ship by Vivien Lougheed / 53

Hounded to the Coast by Bud Osborn / 67

TUNNELS

Sir by Tony Burgess / 85

Valid All Zones by Jonathan Himsworth / 91

THE COMMUTE

7:51 Tozai Line by Heather Watson / 99

Pedestrian by Heather Watson / 101

20 Years of Blank Expressions by Mathew Crisci / 103

Music Note by Ryan Knighton / 113

Space Between Lightning and Thunder (Bowen Island) by Tammy Armstrong / 115

STRANGE RIDES

Blood Transfer by Gregory Betts / 121

My Empty Sleeve by Mark Anthony Jarman / 123

Detached: on the 148 to Ioco by Carla Elm / 131

Retard by Grant Buday / 133

Gifts by M.A.C. Farrant / 139

Have You Ever Been to the P.A. Bus Station? by Betsy Trumpener / 143

Love on a Streetcar by Marian Lydbrooke / 147

Let Your Fingers Do the Walking on the #9 Broadway by Bonnie Bowman / 151

THE DRIVER'S SEAT

Interview with Bob Smith / 161

for all those whose job it is to transport people

INTRODUCTION

The bacteria van, the rolling nut-house, the welfare wagon, the human cattle car. In other words—public transit.

And public transit—the bus, the train, the ferry—is just another way of saying forced proximity, that is, we get to enjoy each others' presence! The suits next to the drunks, the drunk suits slurring into their cells, the children licking the windows, the lovers licking each other, the thugs propping their feet on the seats, the aspiring evangelists practising on a captive audience. On the bus we're nose-to-nose and hip-to-hip, and like it or not we examine each others' scalps, inhale each others' breath, hear each other talk, and watch the mad talk to themselves. And if we're standing we watch for free seats. Is that guy about to get up? Is that woman gathering her bags to leave? We glance around and size up the competition. Or if we're male we wonder if we should offer the seat to the woman next to us? Will it embarrass her? Anger her? And if we offer it to an older person will they be insulted that someone assumes they're infirm? It doesn't matter, because by then the seat's been nabbed away.

As the vehicle lurches from stop to stop, we change grips on the overhead pole because the hand goes numb, reread the ads to avoid eye contact with each other, and try to keep our weight balanced so that when the bus halts we don't plunge face first into the old man wearing a Tilley Endurable hat bristling with a forty-year collection of fishhooks.

Many of us spend ten hours a week on public transit. Let's do the math. Ten hours a week is twenty days a year. On a bus. Torment? Not always. In Turkey, for example, conductors on intercity buses sprinkle orange blossom cologne into everyone's hands to freshen up after each stop.

Riding the bus can be wildly funny or endearingly touching, and I think the range of stories, poems, rants and articles contained in *Exact Fare Only* reflects that diversity. We've included Jean Mallinson's poised meditation on the edifying experience of bus riding in West Vancouver, as well as Tony Burgess's tale about a naked romp through a Toronto subway tunnel. And the pieces range beyond Canada because public transit is worldwide. So you'll find Heather Watson's poem about riding the Tokyo subway, and Vivien Lougheed's memoir about traveling deck-class on a pilgrim ship to Mecca.

And of course, what of the people who work on public transit? What of the drivers and conductors? While bus drivers in Japan wear white gloves, rumour is that here in Vancouver they're all armed. Who can blame them, especially on the Hastings Street run where the weird, the wild, and the woeful make regular cameo appearances. To get the straight goods, we include a selection from Vancouver bus driver Brian Pratt's work journal, plus an interview with driver Bob Smith on how he and his workmates cope in this most public and stressful of jobs.

On a bus in Mexico City one night I recall three guys taunting the driver so mercilessly he taunted them back by taking us all on a suicide ride that made *Speed* look like a turn in a buggy. We careened the entire length of Paseo de la Reforma veering from lane to lane until, having reduced his foes to wimps, he halted then abandoned the vehicle, striding off into the burlap-coloured sunset shouting, "*No mas! No mas!*"

But there will be more. More buses, more trains, more subways, and of course more cars. The more I ride the bus the more I'm convinced the car will never die, and not because it's faster or more convenient or more comfortable, but because it's more private. Cars maintain a separation. Cars isolate us in our own space. Yet on public transit, for all our efforts to remain remote, it's the opposite. On the bus or the train we share space and meet each other whether we like it or not. It certainly provides anecdotes for conversation, and in the case of *Exact Fare Only*, material for literature. That's a good thing.

Grant Buday
Vancouver, September, 2000

REFLECTIONS

Bussing It

Jean Mallinson

A long time ago, when I was twenty or so—the 'or so' indicating that I was at the age when heartbreak seems like a plausible affliction—I was sobbing on a bus, looking out the window, hoping my distress would be less obvious if I did not show my tear-stained face. Then a woman sitting next to me said, "Cheer up, kid, you'll get over it. They're not worth it." Her 'They're' referring to the whole lot of them, whom she dismissed wearily as one who had weighed them all—or a sufficient sample—and found them wanting. At the time, I thought, *How did she know why I was crying?* Now I think, *She was right, he wasn't*, and sometimes I wish I could find her and tell her.

My public tears provided an opportunity for sympathy and advice, but the publicity of busses has its disadvantages: drivers of cars can get behind the wheel in deshabille, barefoot, clad in grubbies, hair unkempt, but bus passengers are relentlessly on view. On a bus at the start of a week day, it is touching to observe the apparel of those dressed for work, how well they have put themselves together, ready to face their world. People do not as a rule groom themselves on busses. I sometimes file my nails in a bus shelter, but put the nail file away when I board the bus. I have never seen anyone take out a pocket mirror and put on make-up in a bus.

The publicity of busses is most poignantly revealed when someone, usually at the end of the day, falls asleep on the bus. Sleep is something people usually succumb to in private, in bed or at least at home. Sleeping adults look and are so vulnerable, so elsewhere, turned into objects, not centres of consciousness looking out at the world: if I see an adult asleep on the bus, I avert my eyes. Sometimes one wonders if the sleeper will wake up in time to get off at the right stop, but there seems to be some chemistry of watchfulness, or some internal compass unconsciously noting the turns and lurches of the bus, for most often the sleeper jerks awake and gets off at his or her stop.

The public space of a bus allows for the display of fashion. It is a pleasure to see a woman well-groomed in the old sense: shoes, gloves, purse and hat matching. One wonders what such an apparition is doing on public transport? Why is she not being driven by a chauffeur? A whole personal history is concealed in the never-to-be-known answer. A life-long habit of dressing continued in spite of altered circumstances may account for her *ensemble* appearance. I sometimes compliment a fellow traveller—but only a woman—on an attractive dress or hat, and I once stretched bus decorum very far when, after admiring a woman's jacket, I asked her where she bought it: alas! It was in Seattle—outside of local bus bounds.

The openness of a bus can be an occasion for embarrassment, most often shared, and caused by a fellow passenger. Most bus riders are aware of the tact required if the journey is to be pleasant. The presence of a traveler—say, intoxicated—whose behaviour is outside the common standards, can cause a busload of distress, followed by relief when the offending person gets off. Uncalled for rudeness, or abuse of authority, as when a driver is sharp with a boarding passenger, or declines some courtesy just outside the rules, can also cause discomfiture. A mother who is rough with her child arouses a similar feeling. No matter if the driver is nearing the end of a bad day, no matter if the mother has more than she can handle. The embarrassment is often mixed with shared sorrow about the human condition, which pushes people to these extremes.

A child on the bus is usually the occasion for a welcome thawing, since a child is not yet part of the unspoken adult contract to keep one's distance. As a writer, I often strike up conversations with the person sitting next to me, and I am usually rewarded by stories of lives I could not have imagined from the outward appearance of the person. My belief that everyone is interesting, everyone has a story to tell, is confirmed by bus or bus stop encounters.

Once, when I was going through a bad patch in my life, a woman I shared the bus stop shelter with told me her husband had "turned homosexual" and left her with two daughters to raise, one of whom had lupus and the other breast cancer. "The good Lord doesn't send us more than we can bear," she told me. She didn't say, "it's good for us," she said, "we can bear it," and I felt instructed. One night on a bus I struck up a conversation with a woman who was learning to paint icons.

She told me that the final stroke in the painting is the speck of white in the eyes of the image. After that, nothing can be added, because the eyes are now looking at you. I used to chat habitually on the bus with a woman who wore a knitted cap summer and winter, who told me how she fed stray cats on her porch and tried to find homes for the kittens. Then I didn't see her any more and it was a bus driver who told me that she had suddenly died.

Busses provide an opportunity for compassion, when a wheelchair passenger—especially if he or she is also paraplegic—gets on. Mixed with the flurry of seat changing to make space, and the watchful anxiety as the person or companion steers the chair into place, is pity, mingled with the sense that no matter what one's trouble may be, the person in the wheelchair clearly has more to cope with. People are abashed by such courage, and get off the bus stepping livelier, feeling lucky.

Travelling by bus affects your sense of time—it speeds up as you get ready to leave the house and walk to the bus stop, knowing that if you forget something you cannot return for it, because the bus, like time and tide, waits for no one. Shutting the locked door of your house to walk to the bus has an instructive finality about it: if you're going to catch this bus, you can't go back. If there is a half hour wait between busses, time slows down and the interval becomes an enormous space to be filled as best one can. I usually read a paperback: the ideal bus stop book fits into purse or pocket, and is absorbing enough to provide a distraction from the anguish of waiting. There should be a noun in English for the state of mind I call "bus-longing." English, unlike German, does not easily come up with these precise compounds.

The bus induces, too, a sense of a time frame imposed, not invented. Skill in deciphering a bus schedule is a discipline for the eye and mind, and no doubt a preparation for reading the other manuals that baffle us as we acquire our various technological devices, each of which arrives with its own arcane User's Manual.

Travelling by bus provides opportunities for extremes of pleasure. The chief rapture is the making of a connection just on time, without the indignity of running, without the tedium of a half hour's wait. It almost restores your faith in the working of things—the government, the universe. The second bus rapture is one I used to indulge in as a child in the back seat of my mother's car: sitting in a timeless daze of daydreaming or making up poems and stories. A bus, especially if you know the driver and are on the way home, engenders a feeling of receptive passivity, of being looked after. In this state on a bus I am often visited by inspirations and insights, solutions to problems. Once, after a house I owned and lived in had been violated by a nocturnal intruder, I got on a bus to escape my house, where I no longer felt safe. As the bus drove over the Lions Gate Bridge, I asked myself what I could do to feel better and I suddenly thought, "I can sell the house." A wave of irrational relief washed over me and by the time we reached the other side of the bridge I knew what I would do. Even though my friends and some members of my family thought I had lost my mind, I went about at once to sell my house and find another. The chemist Kekulé said that it was while riding on top of a London omnibus in the summer of 1854 that, dozing, he dreamed of a whirling serpent biting its tail, an image which gave him the clue to the structure of the carbon chain.

There are at least two maps of any city: the one in the heads of drivers, marked by traffic lights, detours, one-way streets, right and left turns, parking spots, and the one in the heads of bus riders, marked by bus routes and stops. For bus travelers, streets just a block from the bus route are unknown territory, and to be driven along them is a revelation. The streets on the route, in contrast, are utterly familiar, carefully observed through changing seasons. If, because of road construction, snow, an accident or a parade, the bus is obliged to change its route, the trip turns into an escapade, inducing a heady sense of liberation from format. It is no accident that some children's stories are based on the fiction of a bus or a train that decides to ignore its schedule and go off on a wild adventure. One night my daughter, coming home late from a meeting, burdened with things she had to carry, and the only passenger on the bus, was dropped at her door by the bus driver. This miracle was not requested by her, but simply given by the driver, who knew her as an habitual passenger. When she saw him a few days later on another bus, he told her that while he was driving along the quiet residential street where he had dropped her, a late walker called out to him, "What are you doing here?" and he replied, "I'm lost." Then he made the turn back to his route. There is something reassuring about the bus route; it gives a sense that there are things other than natural phenomena that can be counted on.

As well as having different maps of their city, car-drivers and bus travelers have different kinds of travel stories, usually about the difficulties or triumphs attendant on their method of transportation. Drivers go on about traffic, about the impossibility of finding parking space, of the unfairness—to drivers—of one-way streets. Bus riders tell of the heart-break of missing a connection, of the torment of waiting for a bus—I once waited for the Cambie bus for two hours—of standing in the aisle for twenty blocks. The thing is, once you start waiting for a bus, that becomes what you are doing, a kind of passive, self-punitive heroism. You feel, *I have waited this long, if I give up and go home, I've wasted the time I've spent pacing here*, and this admission of defeat seems more unbearable than changing your plans: a kind of crazy determination sets in. One frustration about waiting endlessly for a bus is that there is no way of finding out why it is delayed or when it will turn up. You want to see the thing through, to find out why. While waiting, you feel both mysteriously punished and hopeful against hope, and the relief when you see the bus come into view and read the name on its forehead is one of life's moments of intense gratification, a sense that some drastic dislocation in the order of things has been righted. My image of rescue is not a knight in shining armour but a bus, preferably blue, looming on the horizon.

There are some people you see only when travelling by bus, as if they actually materialize at a bus stop or sitting on a seat as you board. You know they must live in a house, sleep in a bed, have a life, because you hear about it in instalments during bus rides. One woman I have known for over thirty years keeps me caught up on her life during our encounters in transit: who is depressed, who divorced, who is unemployed, how her garden is doing. The close proximity and the little time available seems to encourage these outpourings. When we get off at our separate bus stops, she as good as disappears and I know I have to wait for our next chance meeting to hear the latest chapter in her family saga. Yet we are in a sense old friends, thanks to the curious intimacy of shared confidences while waiting for or sitting on a bus.

One of life's biggest surprises is meeting someone on a bus you know to be a confirmed driver. If you know the person well you exclaim, "What are you doing on a bus?" What catastrophe, what sense of adventure, what desire to go slumming, induced the car-addicted person to board a bus? Such once-in-a-lifetime encounters can lead to small crises: once, shortly after I was divorced, traveling on a bus with my daughter, I observed with astonishment and dismay my ex-husband, never known to use public transport, get on the same bus. My divorce was so recent that I could not see him with composure. Of course my daughter saw him too, smiled, but understood he could not sit with us. What I felt then, more than my own discomfort, was her distress, and a sense that two adults have no business doing this to a child. Since she was old enough to be on a bus by herself, I suddenly remembered, out loud, that I had forgotten to buy peanut butter, and got off the bus at a shopping centre.

Sometimes when I am waiting for a bus in the rain, at a corner without a shelter, and watching cars drive by, the driver and—if there are any—passengers in their private world, I feel envious of their cocoon, their being so sheltered from inclement weather, so in control of their time. But there is something, too, unnatural and insulated about their hermetic enclosure behind glass. I think children who grow up being driven about in cars and never taken on public transport are missing an easily available lesson in human variety, in friendly encounters with well-disposed people outside their close circle.

On balance, the bus is, as the Flanders and Swan song has it, but without their irony, "a transport of delight," a way of getting to know your neighbourhood or your city and of observing your fellow human beings as persons like yourself on the move from somewhere to somewhere else, their heads full of stories, their hearts hoping for someone to tell them to when they arrive.

DIARY OF A MAD BUS DRIVER

Brian Pratt

[ROUTES: 43-130, 1559-2527 & 3-131, 1535-2439—
15/12/97 TO 28/2/98]

Excuse the dashes in place of regular punctuation. This is the way I write notes at work. These stories did not come from a notebook, no one has that sort of time to write more than a few quick bits of info. But I like the form—it reminds me of work—the mad dashes between the lines.

Xmas eve a guy using two canes gets on at Brentwood—no big deal—at Metrotown I want the ten minutes I can get on this run when it's quiet—he's still on—asks how long I will be here—then proceeds to vomit into a plastic bag he has brought with him—it takes most of the ten-minute break for him to finish, to seal the bag and then gather up the rest of his things to leave—I go to the washroom, not the pizza joint, and curse at the walls that this was the Xmas present I didn't want.

New Year's eve—bus service has just gone from regular fare to free service for the rest of the night into the next morning—pick up two young guys—they go to the upper level at the back of the low floor bus—one sits on the driver's side and opens a passenger window that is now at his head level, sitting down—he then proceeds to spit on cars while we are at red lights—we are at a lot of red lights on this trip—I get to watch him spit not once but rapid-fire—spitspitspitspitspit—I hope for an outraged van full of Hell's Angels to board my bus.

An old familiar passenger who rides a scooter shows up at Metrotown on New Year's eve—previously, on the older-style lift equipped buses he was marginal in his skills getting on and off the bus—he employs the point and shoot method of driving a scooter—if he gets wedged in the turn by the farebox he just pushes the throttle harder and hopes to pop through—this time he has a bigger scooter and the low floors have a narrower turn—he can't make it no matter how wide open he jams the throttle—four minutes later (with the help of another passenger, not me because of my back) we have the scooter secured but he is sitting in a seat, not the scooter—he can still walk—getting off I have no sucker to risk their back so I get up to lift the rear of the scooter around the corner wondering if my back will explode and knowing WCB won't cover this injury if it does—bus drivers are not supposed to physically load or off-load passengers—my back does not explode—two hours later I get him returning back to Metrotown.

On my supposed quiet run, on Sunday, in the first five minutes of my week, a guy gets on slightly incapacitated (from what I don't know or care)—he digs in his pocket for something—decides he can dig better in a seat further back—after a few seconds he stops—I look back at him—he says he doesn't have a transfer—I say thanks for telling me—he says sorry—I tell him not to be sorry about something he did on purpose—I still let him ride—he puts his feet up and falls asleep—at the other terminus I make sure he wakes up on the first shake—this technique has been developed over the years—don't stand in front but beside and give his shoulder one good lurch saying loudly "Last stop!"—he shrieks and staggers off—it is debatable whether I want him for a second time on my Monday morning and it is equally debatable whether he actually wanted to go where he is now standing—he walks over to my bus parked away from the stop by the wall and tells me I forgot to give him a transfer—I remind him of our short history together—I remind him loud enough that the driver of the 112 bus leaving the terminus stops to wait to see what's going to happen—my only regret is that the driver behind me probably had to listen to his story about what the last driver did to him.

An almost normal looking woman (everyone is normal until they prove otherwise) barges on at Hastings before I turn up the hill—at the terminus she and another guy who wants some address I barely know the location of are still on—she screams excuse me, you're supposed to go up another two blocks—no, I say, this is the last stop, Cambridge and Grosvenor—no it's not, drive the fucking bus—the magic word—no-one is paid to be sworn at—I say goodbye—that is all I'm willing to say anymore—when she finally pushes off the back door she takes two steps and falls on a lawn—I'm not getting off the bus for her—she gets up and looks at the street signs—then she comes back to the front door of the bus—I'm also not going to open the door up for her—open the door—goodbye—just open the door—goodbye—she comes around to the driver's window which is shut and latched—I just want to apologize—so do it—I'm sorry—fine, goodbye—you don't have to be such an asshole you know—and you don't have to do the things you do, goodbye—somehow the silver tongued devil in the driver seat remembers to point out to the guy who has a street he wants, the direction I think is correct.

I am asked, after my four-minute "break" at the top of Capitol Hill, if I go to Metrotown—I say yes—the passenger tells me transit information told her that I would stop at Brentwood Mall and sit there for thirty minutes before going back up to Capitol Hill—I tell her that I would love a thirty-minute break at Brentwood but I go to Metrotown from Capitol Hill seven times in seven hours—if I get thirty minutes break time it happens over about two hours on the four-to-six-minute instalment plan—but that is the information the public is being given.

She has a blanket draped over her head—and she stinks—the first and only time she rode my bus she sat by the back door—I couldn't figure out where the stink was coming from until it went away when she went away—that's a stink that travelled twenty feet—other drivers told me they won't let her on the bus anymore and the next time I saw her I was out of the seat to intercept and tell her she can't ride—she said she just wanted to go home to take a bath—I didn't believe her—so months later she is in a stop far out of her territory—meaning some poor sap let her ride till then—she seems to be meditating the first three times I stop where she is sitting—I stop for other people—the fourth time I stop she tries to get on the bus—I'm out of the seat again saying I can't have you on the bus—she says I'm having you fired—that still doesn't get her on the bus—I overhear a woman already on ask another woman who just got on why the bus driver didn't let the blanket lady on the bus—the second woman says well she did smell pretty bad—I hear that she ended up in North Vancouver, way outside of her home turf—the driver said the back of the bus reeked of urine long after she had left—she has, as of yet, not followed through on her promise—if that's what it takes to keep her off the bus then that's what it takes.

Two guys with backpacks get on in the industrial lowlands near the freeway—they look like they might have camped there overnight—they don't have enough money to ride the bus—fine—then one asks how they can get to Prince George—I'm hitting the brake as I'm telling him he has to hitchhike on the freeway we just drove over—it's only 750 kilometres away—his buddy, the older guy, laughs and leads the younger guy to the back of the bus—they both play the fool back there until we near the Skytrain station—again the younger kid comes up and asks how they can get to "P.G."?—he's serious—"P.G." is serious for Prince George—I tell him to go down to the Greyhound station and go from there—he says they have no money—I assure him he'll never get from Burnaby to Prince George by city transit within his lifetime—there just aren't those sorts of transfers—I think later I should have put him on the Skytrain for King George Station—a king is always better than a prince—and neither ride the bus.

Another driver a few years ago, during a re-training class, said that it was only five percent of the passengers that caused the problems—no one challenged him on his percentage. On the first day I kept track during this stretch of work—I counted 447 passengers—on my quiet 74—the next two days 427 and 469—four compressed nine plus hour days adds up to 1417 passengers—at one percent there should be fourteen stories for a single week—seventy at five percent—at the maximum for the ten weeks covered here (eight actually, two were holidays) there should be 560 stories—yet another driver, bored at not having to give out change anymore after his first year on the job, started counting passengers—he got to a million fourteen years later—like me he works nights—he figures a day shift driver (A.M. and P.M. rush, mid-runs starting late morning or early afternoon and finishing after the afternoon crush—there are no 9-5 bus shifts), a day-side driver would get their million in seven years—at one percent that's 10,000 problems/stories in as little as a lucky seven years—I used to tell myself I'd stop driving not when I'd seen everything but when I'd seen enough—like with the other lost passengers I have to keep reminding myself we passed that stop way back.

THE DOORS ON THE BUS GO OPEN AND SHUT

TRUE FUNNIES by EVE CORBEL

"That is one **BAD DESIGN**, man"

"**BAD** design"

TO OPEN DOOR STEP DOWN ON TOP STEP

"Oh ya"

This one time I was on the bus and there was this lady—

She had two little kids, one of 'em could walk, and a baby in a stroller.

So she's gonna get off the bus, right,

And she rings the bell and starts dragging everything down to the back.

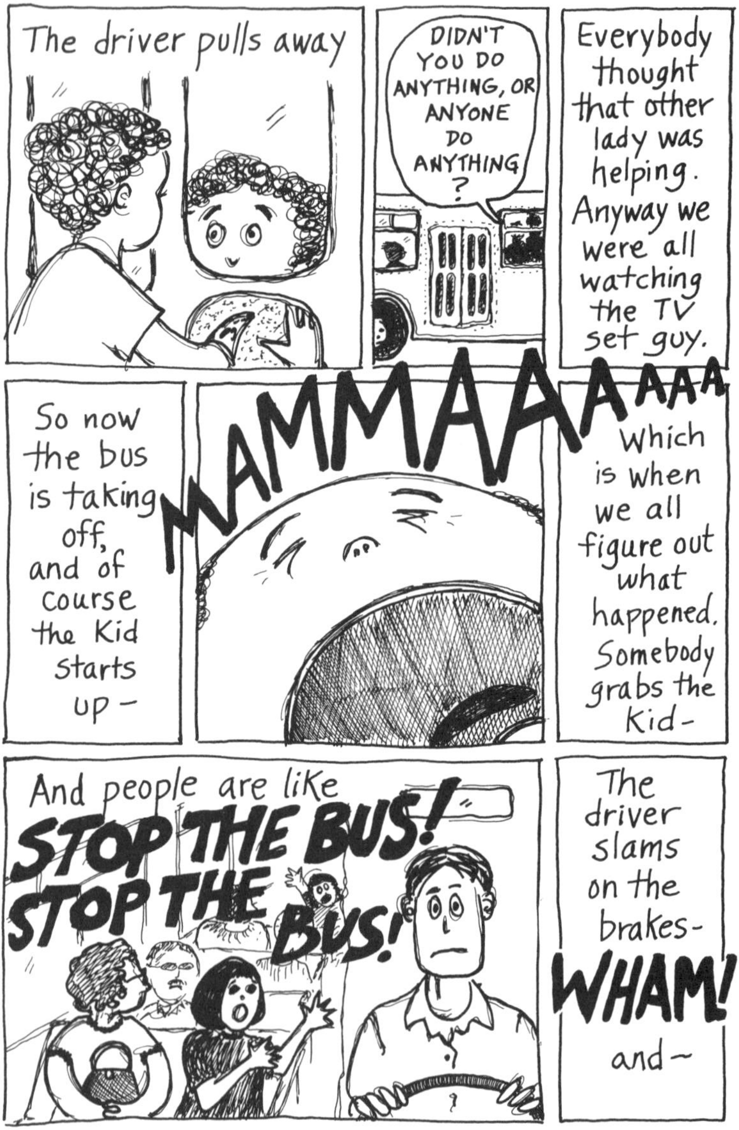

THE DOORS ON THE BUS GO OPEN AND SHUT 35

SMASH

The guy with the TV set goes down.

The mom gets her kid back

There's broken glass all over the floors and seats

And the driver's like

PLEASE VACATE THE BUS.

DID THE OLD GUY GET HURT?

Yeah, but the last I saw of him—

He was sitting on the curb

THE AMBULANCE WILL BE ALONG IN A MINUTE

Ha ha hee hee   Ha ha hee hee   ho ho ha ha ha   hee hee

Laughing his head off 'cuz he knows Transit has to replace the TV and he'll get a way better one.

Like I said, man, bad design. **BAD, BAD** design.

WHERE IT HURTS

Betsy Trumpener

Once, I looked out the streetcar window and saw a man flying through the air. He landed on Queen Street amidst coins from his pocket and his right shoe, which had come off in flight, and I was late for work. I comforted him. I crouched behind him on the road and held his neck stiff, my thumbs along the blade of his jaw, as he called out, *Broken, broken*, to the crowd that had gathered.

I told him that everything was going to be fine, although it was only a guess. I asked him his name. I asked him where it hurt. I said, *Tell me where it hurts,* calm as anything.

The driver who had hit him was chasing dimes along the road. She held them out to us like an apology, *Here*. She was breathing hard. *Don't*, I told her. *Just stop*.

Moments passed, or hours. A policeman leaned out of his cruiser window to say, sorry, he was on his way to a breakfast meeting, but he'd call in the accident. I turned towards the streetcar, its back door still wide open, and called out for a jacket to cover this man on the road. A beautiful fellow came forward and squatted down in front of us, holding a paperback novel in his hands. He offered to help, but he never let go of the book. I can still remember the cover.

Me, squatting on the roadway with the broken man's hair in my hands, and everything all around us stopped.

Later on, after they'd taken him away by ambulance, the police drew chalk marks around where the body had landed. They asked me, *About here?*

About there, I agreed.

The beautiful man with the novel came and sat with me on the sidewalk. I was late for work. I was shaking. He put down his book and took my face in his hands. The streetcar rolled past, like everything was okay again and so I kissed him. And he kissed back, first my top lip and then the bottom. And the first policeman came by, full of breakfast, and said, *Sorry it took so long,* and covered us with a blanket. And even while we kissed, I was shaking, knowing that sometime soon, he was going to put down my face and pick up his book again.

THE FARE

Tim Hearsey

He looked just the way one would expect him to look. Double-knit polyester slacks, plaid shirt and running shoes. A top of the line K-Mart swinger, in all his beige and blue glory, ready to dispel or confirm suspicions. It all began around two-thirty on a wet, mid-week morning. I was sitting in my cab outside the Penthouse nightclub, watching the nocturnal girls squabble and jostle for the few remaining crumbs that stumbled about, just sober enough to pretend they could maintain an erection.

My front passenger door creaked open and I turned to look at the beer-bloated plaid stomach attempting to insert itself into the front seat of Black Top cab 126. Doing the obligatory summation of plaid tummy with my hack intuition, I decided he was good for the fare. I sat silently as the smell of stale cigarettes and ale fumigated the cab, and I waited for his directions. Finally, he spoke, slurring:

"Circle the block."

Deciphering the cryptic meaning behind his directives, I assumed we were to prowl for some girl to relieve him of his DNA. I dropped the flag, shoulder-checked, and pulled across three lanes for a right turn that would begin our circumnavigation of the land of a thousand dates. With hostile gratefulness for any fare at this time in the morning, my eyes scanned the nearly naked trip sheet that gasped a whopping forty-six hard fought dollars. We cruised down Nelson Street past the few remaining sex warriors, parading their hundred dollar cushions that beckoned from the tight confines of latex and satin. As we made a right turn onto Richards Street, my foot slowly pressing the accelerator, he barked:

"Slow down."

Releasing the pedal somewhat begrudgingly, not really wanting to prolong this experience any longer than necessary, I decelerated. In truth, one part of me wished for a reasonably prompt ending and yet, the voyeur in me observed gleefully, craning my neck to catch and savour every last distasteful detail. I stared through the light drizzle of rain that was beginning to speckle my windscreen and with diminishing faith, requested:

"Look buddy, I'm going to need a deposit."

Grunting his disapproval, he stuffed a pudgy little hand into his pocket and pulled out a wad of bills, peeled off a C-note and threw it on the seat, as if to say, who the hell did I think I was to question his integrity. Looking at the brown-faced Queen Elizabeth, who scowled up at me from the tired vinyl, I frowned back. It seemed somewhat surreal that Her Majesty's legal tender maw would facilitate fellatio, fornication and fare. God save her. Feeling especially complicit in this sordid little adventure, I shrugged off my moral quandary and stuffed Liz into my shirt pocket. There would be time later, as I tallied my sheet and counted my tips, to ruminate and analyze my participation.

"Pull over here," my inebriated charge demanded, as he rolled down his window, waving over a particularly sad looking creature.

A make-up spackled face descended and, hovering in the window, began to recite the menu with all the pseudo-happiness of a late night diner waitress. Plaid shirt reached out and ran his hand under her chin, feeling for the rough buzz of fresh stubble.

"Let's go," he ordered, with much disgust. "Fucking queers, godammit!"

Ah, a man of principles, I chuckled to myself and then blanched slightly at the hypocrisy surrounding my own role in this melodrama. But yes, indeed there would be time for those observations later, when I slid the deposit slip of my night's windfall across the counter to the smiling bank clerk.

Around and around we went, in ever-deepening concentric circles, descending into this pit of morbidity. The green digital illumination of the dashboard clock incremented upward, paced by the glowing blue numerals of the meter, as they silently ticked off their mantra—time, money, time, money, time, money. By the end of the first hour of this sojourn, the novelty had definitely begun to wear off. It appeared as though it was a practiced ritual for him, a tolling bell that beckoned, demanding an answer. He seemed to want nothing more than this bizarre form of social interaction. Pulling the car to the curb, eager to end this excursion and hurry back to the safety of the garage, I pleaded:

"Look, I've got to go off shift. I can call you another cab if you want."

I fished for his change with the urgency of a man pretending he has forgotten his wallet when the dinner cheque arrives, casually frisking my pockets.

"I just wanted the company, you keep the change," he said, his voice trailing off with a resigned sigh.

Opening the car door, he deposited himself on the sidewalk. He stood beside the open door for a few seconds and I felt a warm breeze of empathy mixed with the cool, damp early morning air. When the door closed, I hastily pulled from the curb, scurrying back to the lot, a cockroach suddenly caught in the glare of a kitchen light. I watched as he disappeared in my rearview, my skewed ideology shrinking with him. The romantic notion of being a kind of a fisherman on traffic's asphalt sea evaporated quickly, leaving the word "whore" hanging unpleasantly from my mirror like a rancid pine air freshener. I wondered if he had gotten his money's worth.

THE CUSTOMER IS (EVENTUALLY) ALWAYS RIGHT AT BC TRANSIT
OR, AN OPEN LETTER TO MY PASSENGERS ON THE "229 WESTLYNN"

Bob Smith

I would like to apologize in advance to my passengers on the "229 Westlynn." I am going to be a little grumpy for a few days until I work something out, because BC Transit won't let me read on the bus anymore. This is the story:

I've been driving bus for fifteen years. I've got safe driving awards filling a small crate in my garage (BC Transit is very big on awards), and my last accident was back in my rookie season. I like driving a bus, but after a couple of years I found I was getting bored.

I'm sorry, and I'm not sure how to put this gently, but two years of conversations with strangers about the weather and arthritis is a lifetime supply. So, I started to put a book on my transfer rack and found I could grab a paragraph here and there at bus stops and traffic lights.

At some intersections, like Mountain Highway and Lynn Valley, the light is long enough to get through a couple of pages and the traffic jams this summer gave me chapters (bus drivers very quickly develop the peripheral vision of a kindergarten teacher, so I never miss the green light).

Contemplating the beauty of Toni Morrison's prose between stops, or being caught up in a Reginald Hill mystery helped me survive in a job whose only stress was its sameness.

So, for thirteen years there has been a book on my transfer rack, and though there have been many sessions of literary criticism, I never got a complaint—until I moved to North Vancouver last year.

Within three months, on two different routes, I got three complaints phoned in from the same woman. My supervisors and I wrung our hands about the situation. I attempted to be more furtive with the reading. I became more attentive to my passengers. But the book stayed.

Then someone contacted a BC Transit vice-president I had never heard of, and I guess he demanded action. This week my supervisors, in a tizzy, ordered me to take the book off the rack.

Well, what I comtemplate now is this: I figure I've got 16,375 more round trips to drive before I retire. That means I will wait at the Mountain Highway intersection more than 32,000 times. That works out to more than 64,000 unread pages, or all those Russian classics we are forever promising ourselves we are going to read someday. Those, and a truckload of detective fiction.

But then, 64,000 pages probably also represents the combined output of Danielle Steel and Stephen King, so maybe the company is just saving me from myself.

HEAT

Stephen Osborne

It was the first hot day of summer and the bus was full up with people trying not to sweat too much; the air in the bus was heavy and sluggish and conversations were muffled by the heat and the whine and groan of the electric engine stopping and starting, stopping and starting, flattening out time and life as it hauled us slowly forward to our separate destinations. Then a voice materialized in the din, as a woman at the back of the bus said in a clear, confident tenor: "I cried like a baby when he said he was getting a sex change on the telephone." In an instant everyone on the bus became alert. I put down my book and pulled a notecard from my shirtpocket, and the guy next to me and the kid on his knee watched as I wrote down the sentence that seemed still to be resonating in my ears. "I cried like a baby when he said he was getting a sex change on the telephone." I wasn't sure where to put the punctuation. Then the voice spoke again, and the woman said: "His wife was a fat cow like I am, that bovine bitch." I wrote that down too. Only the kid turned around to see who was speaking.

Now everyone on the bus was paying attention to the woman at the back. She seemed to be talking to a companion, but her tone suggested that she was speaking to each of us separately. "I always wanted to be a doctor, you understand, but what I really am is a witch doctor," she said. "He cried like a baby, and what could I do?" I wanted to turn around and look at her then but I wasn't ready to risk making eye contact. She said: "My brothers are all doctors and lawyers and police officers; I wanted to be a doctor too, but with the psychological guerrilla warfare these days, you know what I mean."

The bus continued its passage through the city. I waited with my notecard for the woman to speak again, and when she did I forgot to keep writing. My mind had drifted. When I heard her again, the guy next to me and the kid had disappeared, and the woman was saying, "and then they started that cloning in 1932, this is the fact of it, when Einstein was around, I swear to God I'm related. When you see Billy tell him I got a nose job in case he doesn't recognize me, but I still believe totally in sports. Everyone should do sports, especially gymnastics." The bus had come to a stop, and then it started again and now the voice was silent. Up behind the driver four kids facing each other on the benches were making shapes in the air with their fingers: they were speaking to each other in the language of the deaf. I watched them for a while, unable to comprehend anything they were saying, and then got up and went to the door as the bus came to my stop. I looked down to the rear of the bus and there were three women sitting apart from each other at the back. None of them were speaking. As I stepped down from the bus a man about sixty years old strode past; he was portly and balding and his hands were tucked into the pockets of a lightweight windbreaker. He was leaning forward and saying to a much younger man: "So I slipped the guy a G-note, you know what I mean?" He looked exactly like a mobster in a Mafia movie. I paused and watched him walk down the street with his elbows stuck out. It was the first hot day of summer, and it was much too hot to think.

TRAVELLING

PILGRIM SHIP

Vivien Lougheed

During Ramadan, my friend Kathi Hughes and I were in Egypt, heading for the Sudan and then on to Eritrea. We had already observed some of the more subtle signs indicating the commencement of the holy month. For example, the number of people travelling on boats, planes and buses had doubled. The tea-n-pee breaks during bus trips had been cut in half and the prayer breaks had been lengthened. After dark, however, crowds haunted the restaurants and there was a festive atmosphere on the streets.

We got as far south as Aswan, Egypt when we learned that the overland border between the two countries had just closed. This meant trouble for us. Kathi's visa for the Sudan was valid for another three weeks but mine would expire within three days, and getting another one in Egypt or Sudan was impossible. We didn't have the time to wait for the border to reopen nor did we want to pay for an expensive, last minute flight over the Sudan.

However, when in Cairo, I had heard rumours that there were ships going down the Red Sea first to Saudi Arabia and then on to Sudan. The ports, in other words, were open. It was a long shot but the only one we had.

We raced over to the Port of Suez where we haunted the docks for hours looking for a ship. Finally, a helpful taxi driver took us to a dilapidated building and up a flight of wobbly wooden stairs to an office lit with a 25-watt bulb, heavily veiled in cobwebs. The driver introduced us to a black-bearded man shrouded in greasy, grey robes who was selling tickets for a ship to Port Suakin in Sudan via Jetta in Saudi Arabia. The ship would sail the following morning.

"You must be on time," he warned, carefully enunciating every word. He barely glanced at our passports before handing us our tickets. "There are many pilgrims going to Mecca and you will not get a good place if you are late. You must also tell customs you are in transit or you will not be permitted to pass. The cost is 140 Egyptian pounds, please."

This translated to $60 Canadian, not bad for three day's transportation. We paid. The ticket vendor, handing back our passports, had not bothered to notice that my visa for Sudan would be invalid by the time I boarded the ship. Once back in our hotel room, I took a felt pen like the one that was used to mark my visa, and changed the date from the 3rd of February to the 8th, giving me five more days in which to enter the country. Holding the passport away from my face, I thought the change looked authentic. We would be there in four days.

I then decided to review the Islamic literature I carried with me. I felt that if we were going to spend time amongst the faithful, we had better know what was going on.

"Kathi," I said, opening my book. "Do you want me to read this to you?"

Kathi was busy satisfying her coffee addiction by setting our immersion heater into her tin cup which she had filled with tap water.

"I'd rather you figure out how I'm going to make coffee on the ship," she said. "Since it's Ramadan, there won't be any served in the cafeteria until after dark and I doubt there'll be any electrical plug-ins on deck."

I had no solution for her so I opened my book. Islam, I read, is a word that means to be in a state of submission to Allah. To be a Muslim, or a follower of Islam, one must obey the Five Pillars (basic rules) of Islam.

The first and most important pillar is to declare, in front of witnesses, that Allah is the one and only true God and Muhammad is his prophet. Declaring this fact can be done by anyone at anytime as long as their heart is pure. Although I struggled with the concept of being in a state of submission, the declaration sounded easy to me.

The second pillar is the obligatory pilgrimage to Mecca. We'd be sailing to the Port of Jetta which was just a few miles south of Mecca and I wondered if this would count as fulfilling the second pillar. If it did, we were two-fifths of the way to being good Muslims.

I fell asleep knowing that we were in the last week of Ramadan when it was most holy for Muslims to go to Mecca. The following morning, with the ticket vendor's warning in mind, Kathi and I were up and away by five.

"Without coffee," Kathi kept reminding me as she walked a few steps ahead of me, her running shoes kicking out from her ankle-length skirt. Being a school teacher by profession,

Kathi liked being in the lead. My short legs semi-jogged in an effort to keep up.

"Fasting should help you get into the spirit of Ramadan," I pointed out trying to humour her.

Because we could find no taxis, it took us an hour of walking in the dark to arrive at the port. Surprisingly, we found numerous mile-long lineups similar to those at the BC Ferries during a long weekend. Blowing their horns and inching their way toward the ship were trucks piled twenty-feet high with cardboard boxes, leather luggage, orange plastic water jugs, prayer mats, carpets, and food to be sold or used at Mecca. Every taxi in Suez was in line and crammed with turbaned men or veiled ladies. Air-conditioned tour buses and windowless local transport vehicles were equally as jammed. We looked conspicuous with our heads unveiled, walking faster than the vehicles were moving. We were also the only ones who carried large packs on our backs, small ones on our fronts and plastic food bags in our hands.

In all the chaos we found no coffee vendors.

At customs, men and women were placed in separate lines, thus preventing an accidental encounter of the opposite sex, a definite no-no during Ramadan. Sex is believed to spend energy that should be used for religious contemplation. The lines, separated only by ropes, kept the men and women from physical contact but still left everyone within talking distance.

I would have preferred to be in the men's lineup because they seemed less anxious to get moving. The rotund ladies were aggressive, pushing and shoving to get to the front of the queue. I would not permit a hefty woman with saddlebag hips to shove in front of me. Her husband, in the lineup beside us, said, in English and for everyone's benefit, "Just a minute, just a minute," while he waved his outstretched hands, palms down in a softening motion. Like children listening to their father, the women eased up on their shoving.

Five hours later, Kathi and I staggered onto the triple-decked ship where we found an unoccupied bench and some floor space near the bow on the middle deck. The spot was out of the sun and protected from the wind. We spread our sleeping bags across the bench, tucked our food underneath and waited. It was 11 A.M. when we settled in, three hours past the scheduled departure time.

A wooden stairway beside our bench led to the lower deck where two rows of blue tin showers sat across from a half dozen western-styled toilets tucked into cubicles so small I had to sit sideways in order to fit. The slight odour of urine intermingled with engine oil and the banging of the tin doors when they shut were muffled by the hum of the ship's motor.

From my bench, I looked around and realized we were lucky to have a place to perch even if the benches were in the line of toilet music. On the entire ship, there were no more than half a dozen similar benches and all were occupied.

"There are approximately 1300 people on the boat," an English-speaking crew member told us later that day. "That's about 500 more than the boat was built to hold!"

Still later, as the flood of pilgrims entering the ship slowed to a trickle, the crew member told us that now we would have to wait for the tide to go out so that the ship could sit level with the dock. Then the transport trucks loaded with goods for Mecca would drive into the belly of the vessel. The weight of the trucks would lower the boat and give it more stability in the water.

With good humour, the pilgrims occupied every inch of available floor space, moving here and there, trying to get closer to friends and relatives. The unpainted wooden floors seemed like a hard and dusty bed but the discomforts went unnoticed as the people camped on all three decks, in hallways and on stairwells. Only by locking doors to work areas could the crew keep the pilgrims out. Walking without stepping on someone was a challenge. The festive scene reminded me of Chaucer's *Canterbury Tales* where a Christian pilgrimage doubles as a vacation.

From my bench, I watched three middle-aged Egyptians build a blanket tent reminiscent of a Bedouin camp. They used binder-twine attached to benches and railings to secure three sides and a roof. They then placed their silk mats and embroidered pillows on the floor inside. The entrance to the tent faced us. It was like watching television only we couldn't change the channel.

I opened my book. The third Pillar of Islam describes how, when, and why prayers should take place. This pillar states that a Muslim should face toward Mecca and pray to Allah five times each day. The rituals of standing, sitting, kneeling, bowing and laying strengthens group solidarity. Because mosque floors are flat, everyone stands on the same level. Social status is eliminated.

The fourth Pillar of Islam claims that Muslims should fast (this includes abstinence from smoking) in daylight hours during the month of Ramadan. Pregnant women and nursing mothers are exempt as are the old, the young and the sick. At our ripe age of plus forty, I wondered if Kathi and I qualified as old.

Reading this also made me aware of Kathi, who was on the

prowl, looking for electrical plug-ins and peering at peoples' baggage for signs of coffee making equipment. As mid-day prayers commenced, Kathi joined in solidarity with a man, a Sudanese, who looked ragged and out of place among the pilgrims. His name was David and he had an addiction to cigarettes. Kathi, a non-smoker, was unable to help him.

Many of the pilgrims were just as restless as David and Kathi, waiting to break the Ramadan fast. Some sat with their water glasses perched near their mouths as if sniffing the odourless liquid could quench their entire day's thirst. Nicotine addicts clenched unlit cigarettes between their teeth and clutched lighters in their fists. Occasionally I spotted someone surreptitiously slip a morsel of food into his or her mouth.

Hunger was no problem for Kathi and me. All day we hid behind our propped-up gear and snuck meals of fresh vegetables chopped into pita bread and washed down with sips of mineral water.

"Coffee, please Allah," Kathi repeated once every hour until evening when she also sat facing west, watching for the sun's yellow disk to melt into the ocean. When the earth was finally cloaked in darkness, she joined the long lineup of people (mostly men) in the cafeteria. Many of our fellow passengers shared her addiction.

Kathi returned from the cafeteria sipping a cup of steaming coffee.

"It's instant but better than nothing," she sighed, plopping down beside me, her gnarled fingers clutching the container. Kathi's hands and feet, slightly deformed at birth, give her the appearance of having severe arthritis. This, along with deep laugh lines that streak her ruddy cheeks were an asset on the boat as it made her look old enough to be respected like a parent by young Muslims.

"I noticed on the top deck that there are numerous tent families similar to ours," she said nodding toward the men across from us.

"There's also a room around the back of the boat that has about 200 padded seats," I informed her. "All occupied."

For the pilgrims, the sunset breakfast was followed by prayers and chanting which were followed, much to my surprise, by hours of socializing. The few deck lights added a glow of warmth, taking away from the cold black that had fallen over the Red Sea and the loneliness of the few lights still glowing on shore.

While watching the crowds of heavily clad people mill around the ship, I wondered if Muslims generally knew how to swim. I knew that in the event of an accident, the few lifeboats available around the ship could not hold all the people on board. "Jump in first and swim away from the crowd," I chanted to myself.

Although to us this was a unique and exciting experience, we too were a unique and exciting experience to the pilgrims. The women often stared boldly, but the men usually took sideways glances at us so that no suggestion of sexual desire could be implied. But during that first day, no one tried to approach us.

At midnight, the ship blew its whistle, a sharp blast that got the attention of all on board. Many leaned over the rails to watch as the boat began to glide silently along the golden road formed by the half-moon glistening on the dark water. It was nineteen hours since we had gotten up to catch the boat before it left without us. I was tired.

Knowing that sleep would not come easily with all the excitement of finally sailing, I watched my tent family. One of the men had a wide girth, grey beard and skinny legs which poked out from under his skirt-like robe. His balding head was covered in a white crocheted skullcap and he kept a smile between his pudgy cheeks. Obviously he was pleased with his pending journey. I watched as he lay in his tent, upon numerous pillows with his head resting on his forearm that was propped on the floor. I called him Lawrence of the Boat. An older man sat next to him, cross-legged and stiff, puffing on a cigarette. I presumed he was the father of Lawrence.

Lawrence had a chunky wife clad in a white head-covering which she constantly flipped over her shoulder in an attempt to keep it in place. She was there to serve both men, a position she seemed to enjoy. I nicknamed her Chattel, putting emphasis on the second syllable to make it sound French rather than judgmental. Before each prayer session, Chattel tugged at the curled points of the men's shoes to remove them from their feet. From an orange plastic jug she then poured fresh water over their hands and feet so they could perform their obligatory pre-prayer cleansing. Later, when the men returned to the pillows, Chattel would replace the shoes. She also shooed flies from their faces with a horsehair whisk, prepared and served their breakfast, and lit their cigarettes. While I watched, an odour of bitter instant coffee and potent burning tobacco, softened by the salt-laden air, invaded my nose.

As the ship cut through the dark, people began eating the night's second meal which seemed to be the most festive. This meal ended at about 1:30 A.M. Preparations for the final meal began immediately. It was served at 4:00 A.M., just before sunrise and early morning prayer. Needless to say, our first night on the ship was sleepless.

After sunrise, I lay on my bench and looked around as the pilgrims settled onto their mats for a good day's sleep. Many covered their faces to block the sun. David, the Sudanese man who had introduced himself earlier, hung over the railing across the deck from us, covertly puffing away on a butt he'd picked up on the stairwell.

I opened my book, hoping those who understood English would see that I was studying Islam. The fifth Pillar, I read, is that of charity. Accumulation of riches was a no-no. This was an easy pillar for me. I'd never have riches because I gave all my money to airline companies in exchange for tickets to foreign places.

The impulse to roam started when I was a kid in elementary school. Lacking any fear, I explored the streets of Winnipeg on my bike until the tires wore out. At eighteen, I hopped a Greyhound and discovered the Canadian mountains where exploration became my specialty. Eventually I moved on to explore foreign lands, always compelled to go to places others had not been, where there was danger or war or deprivation. I was one of the first to enter Communist China in 1983 when limited, independent travel was finally permitted. Because there was nothing else available at the time, I had to carry a missionary's Mandarin dictionary, pointing at phrases like *revival meeting*, hoping this would get me a hotel room. Now, with a forged visa, I was going to Sudan.

David, when he found out our destination, tried to discourage us. As the pilgrims slept and the ship slid through the calm water under a cloudless sky, he told us his story. He was a Christian who had entered Egypt without a visa or passport for the purpose of raising money to purchase arms for the rebels who were fighting against the ruling class Muslims in northern Sudan. He had been caught and sentenced to twelve years in prison. His rat- and flea-bitten skin was a dark contrast to the unblemished cleanliness of the pilgrims.

"I'm not a Christian," I told him after he described some of the horrors suffered by the followers of Jesus. "More an agnostic."

"Even worse," he said. "No religion is the ultimate sin."

Kathi walked toward us, her short red hair looking brassy and obtrusive among the covered heads of the pilgrims. I must look just as conspicuous, I thought, letting my hand pat my hair unconsciously.

"I've got nothing to lose so I'm going back to fight some more," continued David. "My parents were killed by the Muslims and I won't take a wife until we have peace."

After a bit more conversation, I slipped quietly across the deck to my seat where I had my Dickens novel hidden under the cover of my book about Islam.

By the end of the day, the fifth Pillar of Islam, charity to travellers, fell on me like the salt towers of Gomorrah. After sunset, while Kathi was trying to consume a day's supply of coffee in one sitting, I was restlessly walking from one end of the ship to the other, stepping over people perched on the stairs, in the hallways, and on the decks.

Pulling at my arms and skirt, and refusing to accept my "no" for an answer, a group of ladies insisted that I join them. Feigning enthusiasm (I had been nibbling, secretly, all day) I partook of cabbage rolls stuffed with curried rice, chicken pieces painted in spicy sauces, pickled carrots cut into geometric designs and cold string beans that had no flavour at all. The women competed with each other by tugging at my skirt and nodding their covered heads, seeking my approval. By accepting charity rather than giving it, I was helping these people get to paradise.

Finally, on the third day of sailing, the horizon's solid line was broken by a glistening stone pillar, red in colour. We were still too far away to see a town. A woman holding a child grabbed my arm and pointed.

"Jetta," she sighed. "Mecca," she sighed again.

The pillar marked the entrance to the Port of Jetta.

As we approached land, the pilgrims started getting ready to go to Mecca. Between prayers, women showered. The tin stalls had turned slimy from the excessive soap used by the pious before prayers. Concealed from the men after showering, the women rebraided their hair and then hid the braids under white head-veils. They also concealed their female figures inside black, ankle-length overcoats, called chadors, which I imagined to be insufferably hot under the tropical sun. Some ladies were shrouded in head-to-foot chadors that hung over their faces and left only netted slits for their eyes. Even hands were covered in black gloves tucked into the sleeves of their robes so not a single skin cell was showing.

The men also had special outfits to wear to Mecca. Each wrapped a white, seamless sheet around his waist, skirt fashion, and a second sheet, toga-style, over one shoulder. The sheets were held in place with safety pins. I was told that all Muslim men were equal in the eyes of Allah, so in Mecca all dressed the same.

Everyone ran frantically up and down the stairs from one deck to the next, exchanging words or borrowing forgotten items. The tent family busily prepared to disembark. While Chattel of the Tent was showering and changing, the men had to look after themselves. They fussed and fidgeted, trying to help each other, moving pins from one spot to another and then back again. They barked and shouted until Chattel heard them and returned to fix both of their garments. She did this in a flash and with a scolding.

As we docked, groups of men, robed in their togas, paraded around the ship singing hymns and chanting prayers. They stopped occasionally, knelt, and touched their heads to the floor while facing the direction of Mecca. One lady pointed to a man with a callous on his forehead and explained that the callous was a sign of great faith and had been put there by God.

The air was electric with anticipation and excitement. Kathi was electric with want of caffeine. I imagined what it must be like with two million devout followers circumnavigating the Ka'ba not far from where the ship was docking. It would give the people a real sense of solidification.

As the ship eased into its berth, three educated women who spoke English mustered up the courage to speak with me. They tried to entice me into becoming a Muslim and going to Mecca with them. They thought my conversion would give me true happiness and help pave their way to heaven.

"No visa for Saudi Arabia," I explained. "But I assure you that I'll consider becoming a Muslim." I showed them my book. They smiled, taking my word as a promise.

As hordes of people started moving towards the gangplank, I noticed a cripple with a crutch having difficulty getting his bag to the stairs. I went over and carried his meagre possessions for him, much to the astonishment and approval of those nearby. I had upheld one of the Pillars of Islam with my act of charity. If they only knew, I thought, how Kathi had also held up a pillar by abstaining from coffee each day.

Maybe as a reward, we would get through the Sudanese border without the authorities noticing the changed date on my visa.

Pushing my fears into the back of my head, I stood at the rail and watched the people enter Saudi Arabia, an oil-rich country which does not offer cheap vacations for pilgrims. I thought that among all his other accomplishments, Muhammad was probably the first and greatest tour operator in history.

HOUNDED TO THE COAST

Bud Osborn

'**W***e're on a hiiigggh-way to hell!*' screams across the narrow aisle out of a ghetto blaster held by young jailbird tattoos.

Wild white boys piling into the rear seats.

'Sixty-nine hours to Vancouver,' the ticket seller had said.

Janice, a brand-new parolee, flops into the empty seat beside me. The judge exiled her from Toronto for two years, to Thunder Bay. Paroled to parents she hasn't seen in six years. She's drunk and showing off her slit-pocket booster-coat. Handing out valiums and passing a bottle of rum.

All I can think of is Marie, abandoned in a hell-hole hotel of drunken emergencies. But I was on the verge of jumping from the window there, or throwing someone else through it.

Silver comet splits the darkness, outside Sudbury.

A monstrous paper mill's blowing Bhopal-like clouds near Espanola. The hyper-anxious doctor's son who drank his way out of university, gets off at a blacked-out station, and heads for a bar before calling home.

Anthony, a passenger I meet at a rest stop, lets me know that Janice has told the old Frenchman who's been bugging her that I'm her pimp. I conjure grim scenarios . . . .

Anthony's a blues musician making his eighth trip to the coast in ten months. Says he doesn't know why, just knows he can't stop.

The woman in the seat ahead of me, who climbed aboard in Sault Ste. Marie, says she's been in Toronto, and is going to Winnipeg to see her ex-husband, though her fiancé is waiting for her in Saskatoon. Somewhere along the way she ended up hitchhiking, a biker picked her up, gave her a ride and a ticket for this bus.

A girl from Costa Rica, an exchange student, fills a cup with water from the toilet tap, and appears startled and confused when a man warns her, 'Don't drink it, it's poison!' and a woman advises her, 'It's not really poison.'

The kid with the blaster and tattoos said he woke up drunk, rolled, and broke, in Buffalo. He lifts the white plaster cast covering his wrist and forearm more like a badge of honour than a flag of surrender.

Janice broadcasts a tabloid headline to the entire bus: 'Man solves his own murder!'

Another woman's reading a Pentecostal magazine. The man sitting next to her is reading *Hustler*.

Lake Superior, past Dead Horse Creek—trees . . . trees . . . trees . . . and glacial rock.

Bleak houses in battered White River, advertising itself as 'The Coldest Spot in Canada,' for once hitting seventy-two below.

Wild boys making noise and smoking. The driver pulls onto the highway shoulder, walks to the rear and tells them, 'There's not going to be any partying back here!' A wild boy blames Janice, 'She keeps tryin' to show us her boobs!' And Janice says, 'Hey, driver! They're just givin' you the grease!' Through the window I see the 'World's Largest Oilcan' in Moosonin.

Amethyst Mines in Thunder Bay, Marie's astrological gem. A charm against drunkenness.

Old black and tan dog lying in the middle of a sunlit oil-stained bus bay. The nervous wide-blue-eyed novice missionary, who replaced Janice next to me, is on his way to a Native reserve. He stares at the dog and says, 'Boy, he isn't worried about anything, is he?'

In the station, a newspaper headline shouts: 'Cannibals Shrink Space Alien's Head!'

This is called a 'non-smoking fresh-air bus,' jam-packed and sour with stale sweat.

A new driver threatens, 'Don't smoke in the restroom, or I'll put you off the bus!' Smokers roll pop cans below the seats, rattling and clanging all the way to the driver's heels. Somebody yells, 'Let's put the driver off the bus!'

Lung-wracked coughing careens throughout the Greyhound, sounding like a mobile quarantine unit for some respiratory plague.

A pond with a large beaver lodge resting peacefully in it, beautiful with smooth sticks and mud . . .

A sign proclaims Niponee to be the home of Al Hackner, a curling champion.

The newest hound-boss admonishes the wild boys, 'I don't want you disturbing the other passengers!'

'They're disturbin' us!' a wild boy replies.

Riding in early grey afternoon . . .

'So you're the new driver,' a wild one says. 'Good, the last driver was drunk!'

A lengthy general discussion concerns cross-country welfare benefits. Which towns and cities let go of emergency cheques, or a meal, or an overnight flop.

A wild boy tells the conservatively dressed older man next to him, 'I trust you. You don't look like me. I know what I'm like.'

A black man reading a Reggie Jackson biography turns to a jabbering wild boy and says, 'You might notta been talkin' to me, but you mighta been talkin' about me!' And silences the boy with a hard stare.

Roadside rock like a petrified rainbow: blue, green, grey, white, black, yellow, red . . .

We stop at the Terry Fox Statue Lookout. A plaque reads: 'He left a challenge for each to meet in his own way.'

A very drunken man reels aboard, and soon reveals the contents of his travelling bag, nothing but Alcoholics Anonymous literature. He says he just got out of a treatment centre.

My thoughts turn to Marie, again and again. Watching the full moon fiery white in the clear sky, I imagine its light shining into her window too. And, as though it's a telepathic satellite, I bounce a prayer off the moon, expressing my hope for renewed love, to Marie.

On the restroom blackboard in Upsala, someone's written: 'Louie, your moose is tied up in Savant.'

Itinerant welders. Drywall workers. Tunnel labourers. Riding west, hoping for jobs. A fresh start . . .

At a rest stop, I opened a free copy of *Plain Truth* magazine, and learned that 'Greed is the underpinning of human nature.'

A small news sheet I picked up at a restaurant in the Soo reported that a seventeen-year-old female university student had been stabbed to death.

Twenty-five kilometres from Dryden, an inverted pentagram's painted on a boulder. A symbol for Satan . . .

Wild boys even louder, and nastier. Completely broke now, living on water and crackers.

It's Credit Union Day in Dryden. An enigmatic sign commands: 'Share the Vision.'

A cold-hearted white moon hangs over Kenora's Native miseries.

The wild boys were evicted as soon as we entered Manitoba. Furious, full of grievances, they threatened the driver, cursed Greyhound, and were left standing in a parking lot, impotently shaking their fists.

Morning sunlight flashes off Little Steel River. Short-ride Indians sit silently.

The young missionary from Pennsylvania's reading a paperback entitled *Witch Doctors and Sorcery*. One brief tale I skim involves a priest the Indians disliked enough to put a curse on him, so that whenever he tried to preach to them, he lost the ability to speak.

Before disembarking, the blond missionary was chewing his fingers and staring grimly at the road ahead.

Mostly poor people ride this bus that stops at expensive restaurants. An order of toast between two children. An orange between two hungry adults. Other passengers wait until diners have left their tables, then scoop the leftovers.

Stark sub-zero silvered pine tree in bone-blown Manitoba. Lone raven on a bare branch . . .

The ex-Vietnam vet behind me told his seatmate, a kindly looking elderly woman reading a Bible, that he just got out of a hospital. She asked what was wrong with him. He said, 'I thought the devil was chasing me. My psychiatrist told me a lot of people think that.'

I sink, self-pityingly, into my seat, like the stone sinking into my gut then pray Marie and I will be together soon—but saner, sober, and aware that we may not be on earth solely to make each others' lives sheer hell.

She and I detonate the deepest terrors in each other, unheal the oldest wounds. Being with each other is often like treading a minefield planted with bombs of trauma. Marie's family remained together no matter what violence they wrought upon each other. My family fled separately after each new explosion of rage and madness.

Marie and I grew up with murderers, suicides, alcoholics,

drug addicts, thieves, convicts, mental patients, and rapists.

I remember my grandmother's summarizing statement, when told a distant relative was compiling a genealogy: 'Why'd he want to do that? The ones we know about's bad enough!'

Oh dear God, help Marie and me overcome ourselves.

Approaching Winnipeg, I see the Place Louis Riel spelled out in letters of fire and recall the Walt Whitman Hotel in degraded downtown Camden, New Jersey. Two poet-prophets of North America—exclusive hotels.

Night of insomniac hell, switching buses, and beside me a guy sleeping like he's digging a puck out of a corner. Elbows flailing.

Red-orange sunrise near Regina. Volcanic sky-island surfacing from snow-fields. Light-blue fog. Pale lavender horizon.

Another ten-minute rest stop. Anthony says he feels 'ridiculous,' forty-two years old, riding a Greyhound back and forth across the country, with a copy of Kerouac in his back pocket.

I tell Anthony my terrible blues with Marie. 'Maybe you really love her,' he says. 'I do!' I tell him passionately. Our five years together reeling kaleidoscopically through my mind.

Five years of depressions, trances, addictions, starvations, mangled surgeries, desperation, tears and blood bursting from both of us—feeling doomed; but also joyous laughter, and intimacy such as only survivors from the worst of tragedies can feel, and our acts of selfless love, sometimes even recognized as such by the other.

An older woman in front of me explains to her seatmate her reason for riding Greyhound: 'My husband's almost totally deaf. So you don't talk unless you absolutely have to. And when you just sit around and look at the walls, and watch TV and read, I said, I'm going to Vancouver to stay with my son for a while.'

Anthony says he's been through the rock-pop Holiday Inn studio-trip, and just wants to play the blues now. As soon as he can get off the highway.

He knows individual waitresses by now in these bus stop diners, and whether to trust a meal, or just order soup.

In Regina, he had an epiphany, declaring unequivocally that our waitress had 'the world's plainest brown dress.'

Riding another long night through, awake and aching, with lives thrown like dice down the highway . . .

In Tompkins, Saskatchewan, half-a-dozen ranchers board with their wives. Beginning a hound tour like they did ten years ago, to Las Vegas, San Diego, and Tijuana.

'Three weeks in all. You only live once,' said the tall rancher beside me, with large sun-darkened hands, bulging forearms, a brown leisure suit with small Canadian flag lapel pin, cowboy boots, and a white Stetson hat.

'A strange thing happened this year,' he said. 'It rained all of September. Half the grain rotted.' He couldn't recall that ever happening before.

He said it was a good summer for him, but, 'There were a lot of closures for anyone started a farm or ranch in the last ten or fifteen years. They don't have a chance,' he said, softly, looking down at his hands, his face squeezed with compassion for men like those we see hanging out in prairie bus stations.

Hostile and curious looks from men in their thirties and forties 'who don't have a chance . . .'

A stop near Outlook, and I imagine the fierce blue-gold sky-wind roaring across the vast land blowing chains from my spirit and senses.

The old rancher keeps a diary. Spying over his shoulder, I read last night's entry: 'Rough night. Kept moving. Turning.'

Anthony complains about contemporary music, that it has become as colourless and moulded as 'ice cubes in a plastic tray.'

'Change the way we pray' is the last entry I read in the rancher's diary.

In Swift Current, a good-natured Italian tourist camera bug who's been stalking the aisle for photo opportunities, lugging all manner of camera paraphernalia, shooting out of the window, was attacked by an old man in the first seat by the door. He apparently thought the Italian was taking a picture of him, and drilled the camera lens with a right hook, but failed to knock out the exuberance of the Italian, who has provided comic relief, trapping himself in the Greyhound crapper, and struggling with the door for several minutes before extricating himself, red-faced and grinning, to be greeted by laughter and applause from the rest of us.

Someone surmised the old man became so offended by the camera because he was probably in the Witness Protection Program. I thought perhaps the old man subscribed to the belief that the artificial reproductive capabilities of the camera diminishes the spirit, or steals the soul of the person photographed. Most likely, the extrovert Italian just got on his nerves.

The Italian chose this Greyhound route specifically so he could take photos of the Rocky Mountains, but was rendered speechless when informed we'd be passing through the mountains in the dead of night.

Reflection of a tree, dark-blue, floats amidst mountain shadows, in the middle of a pond, in Alberta.

Now that the Italian has recovered from his shock about crossing the Rockies in darkness, he's photographing people in doughnut shops and restaurants.

A young guy in the seat beside me has been guzzling bottle after bottle of codeine-laced cough syrup. I recently read that Canadians consume more codeine per capita than people in any other industrialized country.

I have certainly done my damnedest to help Canada reach the top in that category. Over-the-counter Tylenol with codeine just about killed me. I ended up taking lethal dosages to prevent withdrawal sickness from the codeine, and consequently overdosed on the Tylenol.

In the emergency room, a nurse told me Tylenol overdoses were common. Two doctors appeared, looked at my test results on a clipboard, and gaped at me with open mouths. Then one of them blurted a question I've been asking myself for most of my life: 'Why are you still alive?'

All I could do was hold up my hands.

Outside Medicine Hat, twenty years ago, were trailers with showers and bunks and hot food, provided free for road-weary travellers by the federal government. Today in Medicine Hat, it's twenty cents to take a shit, plus graffiti: 'Fuck You And Everyone That Looks Like You!'

Twenty years ago in Medicine Hat, a very old Indian woman walked past me on the sidewalk, stopped and turned to face me. She stood there looking into my soul, it felt like, and her eyes began pouring tears.

She walked slowly up to me, and when quite close, thrust a two-dollar bill into my hand, and said, 'My heart is sad for you.'

I stood there, astonished, as she walked away.

So many empty, abandoned houses throughout the forests and prairies, near small towns, on open land, with no way for anyone to live in them. People forced by economic techniques into urban pressure cookers.

Greyhound drivers drinking coffee in a restaurant, talking grievances filed, breakdown schedules endured . . .

Calgary's lights at night, spread alluringly like petals and tendrils of a bright carnivorous flower.

Horrific farting turning the hound-bus into a gas chamber. I finally passed out, and woke up sweating.

'Emergency exit . . . Lift this bar . . . Push window open.'

I look around at my fellow passengers trying to sleep, wrestling with themselves in their seats. No contortionist performance artist I've ever seen has executed such excruciating postures as we do, trying to fit comfortably into these impossibly cramped seats.

I snatch a newspaper from the floor and read that a psychiatrist has announced the first conference to study and discuss: 'Self-mutilation . . . more common than you think . . . discovered like bulimics and multiple personalities . . . people ashamed to admit it . . . covered by clothing.'

No revelation to me. I've swallowed and inhaled poisons, stabbed needles into my veins, slashed razor blades across my arms, and purposely driven an automobile into a wall at sixty miles an hour.

I've known people who pour acid on themselves, eat broken glass, stick their fingers intentionally into light sockets, viciously bite themselves, shoot bullets into their feet and practice various other disfigurements—inflicting lacerations and burns—as though attempting to mortify some unspeakable, shameful experience. And yet I've heard of religious people who wear hair shirts, put sharp stones in their shoes, or wear belts with nails embedded in their flesh.

But then, the religious do that in order to be reminded of God. The rest of us do that to be reminded of ourselves.

A sign says: 'Mountains.' Wet rock beside the highway . . .

At Banff, young ski-resorters crowd the bus. I'm tired, anxious, stinking, and they seem to me prattling, puffed-up, pretentious, cream-filled beings who've never missed a meal in their lives. My judgmental attitude bugs me more than they do.

The communion between Marie and me, at the last moment, as I was leaving for the bus station, comes back to me as something miraculous.

No matter how frustrating trying to love and receive love has been for us, we re-sealed a deep connection that drew us to each other in the first place.

Marie called me 'friend' more fervently—and with such a radiant expression—than I've ever received from anyone.

Then we embraced, outside hotel hell, where guardian angels hovered over us.

A banner at the Mohawk gas station in Golden says: 'Reward Yourself.' But it doesn't say for what.

Headline in a Yellowknife newspaper: 'Drunks disrupt assembly.' They'll do it every time.

Heavy rain falling . . .

'I'm Chinese, sorry, I don't speak English,' says a man in suit and tie, to a cowboy who replies, 'That's okay. A lot of people in Canada don't speak English.'

I smoke a cigarette in the rain at Hope, where *Rambo* was filmed. That movie's inspired a loner-army of camouflage-dressed psychotics, committing mayhem in neighbourhoods and on city streets throughout North America.

Should be some kind of victims' commemorative plaque, or at least a marker reading 'He left a challenge . . .'

Closing in on Vancouver. Crowded-bus-rush-hour-torture.

Humpty-Dumpty, the businessman, is wedged beside me, squirming with boils on his ass, he tells me. My own spinal fractures are biting me with sharp teeth.

I have come out here to die—like how many other Greyhound refugees, burning a continent behind them?

I've come here to die, either ignominiously in some wretched situation, or to my old life. But this is it. Nowhere left to run except into the ocean.

And Marie said she too would be riding the 'hound to Vancouver, to me, when she was ready . . .

Heljo, a friend of Marie's and mine, and the woman who paid my fare out here, was driven, terror-stricken, through bomb-wracked Europe during the Second World War. Heljo, from Estonia, was more than once buried alive with debris, shattered bricks, and scorched wood, but survived to build a new life in Canada. She told me she believes Marie and I will rise like 'mated phoenixes.'

Hounded to the coast, by furies and angels . . .

Hounded to the coast, to annihilation or resurrection . . .

Lunar eclipse. Skyline. Green dawn.

TUNNELS

SIR

Tony Burgess

It seems to me that there are only two kinds of stories. The first, and conventionally the best kind of story, is one which you relate to. It is a story that, given the right variables, we imagine that any one of us might have told. *The Executioner's Song* is a good story; the lie that Gary Gilmour told to buy himself some time so he could rob a gas station and shoot two people is not. The second type of story is bad and, I think, it is the one we most often tell.

A friend has just told me a story. And I am going to try to relate it in a way that redeems him, makes him sympathetic; though, I assure you it was not told to me that way. I am going to pollinate a bad story with a good one, and so I have to tell you first off, that he is gainfully employed. I'm not sure exactly what he does, but I know when he gets hired, it's so that he can tell the company what they should do, not the other way around. It matters a little, because I want you to understand that he is a person who has a few things at stake. A good job, responsibility, that sort of thing. If a person doesn't gamble with at least that much then what's the point? My friend gambles with a life based on skill and ability and earning power and relationships. He's attractive, funny, clever, a bit nearsighted, slightly affected, feminine. He is shocked by the selfishness of characters on television, and flutters his eyes when he's nervous. I think he's a marvelous fellow. He is always returning to girlfriends who destroy him and he is so sensitive about this ill treatment at the hands of his lovers that he is terrified of heterosexuality. He loved the Psychedelic Furs. He loved Gary Numan. Bauhaus. He was so upset that David Bowie's *Heroes* was being used in a commercial that he wept. Now that I think more about him, I think that I just love him.

Isn't it reassuring that people feel things like this? I mean, my god, forget about how little you care about the things he does, the people he does. Dancing like an idiot, his arms waving like he's one of Don Ho's dancers, handsome, too, his lips babyish, he pokes a finger pushing his glasses up his nose. He is jealous of the careers of artists. Giving in to moments of weakness, bitterness, correcting the grammar of acceptance speeches, he loves gorgeous and obscure things, doesn't take the 'message' of anything lightly, but believes that all gravity must be earned, must be elegant, must really be about things turning on themselves. And he loves movies. David Lynch, but only too much David Lynch. He is affected by movies. Truth is, affectation is his second nature and you're not allowed to be cruel about this. He whistles after a good movie. He stops and looks at things. *Paris, Texas* made him wander aimlessly. *Edward Scissorhands* made him feel girlish, petulant. He seeks out the friends who let him be a girl, because he knows, the faint, the fan is always young, always female. All of his ex-girlfriends have turned these qualities back on him, in mid break-up, stabbed him, conspired against him.

Oh well. We're not going to do that. He comes out of the movie house and wants to sing. He stands in a glassed-in enclosure, sings in falsetto. People walk by, he stops. Makes a little pervert face when they've passed. A light bulb pops over his head, and he steps quickly down to the Museum Subway stop, then, humming, mouthing a word, he clatters on sharp blue heels down. He keeps the song in his head, keeps it going like this, making no eye contact, not noticing if anyone notices him. On the platform, he hurls his voice up the tunnel. Rich and beautiful, this is how his singing voice should sound. He keeps singing, restraining the voice, holding back, saving it all for the finish, something improvised, something just for tonight. The platform is empty, but he's resolved that if anyone did come down, or a train came by, he would keep singing. Loudly, earnestly, well sung. He strolls, Maurice Chevalier now, to the end of the platform, and steps down the grimy stairs, hidden there, little emergency crew steps, his body is turned outward, open to the audience, and his hand floats out as he descends, opens up and the fingers snap sharply, and point as he skips out between the rail. As he walks along the tracks, he feels the black spaces between the pillars between him. He hears them in his voice, and as the platform disappears he is covered in a patina of black grit. For the finish he hops up on the cover over the third rail, and turns to the glow coming from the platform. The note he holds—his entire upper body holds it—is superb. He growls softly and closes his mouth. The song is over, he stands with an outstretched white plastic bag. White T-shirt, khaki shorts and dark blue sandals, luminous, alone. He has done his subway repertoire. Depeche Mode, Home (from *Ultra*) Martin Gore's cover of "never turn your back on Mother earth" (from *Counterfeit*) a minor key jazz version of *My Favorite Things*.

Just south of Museum Subway where the north and south tracks are separated by cement pillars and partitions, a little further on, beyond yellow barriers, this median structure suddenly opens up—what he describes as a chasm; and having gone this far, having sung so loudly, (where is everyone? where are the trains?) he decides to turn in at the barrier and walk, his heart skipping, into the strange dark hall. The smell. Leather? A train set? A train. He stands still as the sound of the train crashes around him, both sides, both ways. Light shuffles the shadows around him. Then the end sucks past north and south. He turns and runs south behind the train, then bounces up between two pillars. His heart is pounding, these are exciting days. No one knows. He is panting, and he has an erection. So he removes it and looks down. These things seldom meet. The long-suffering surface of this pillar, soot accumulation, and this, he bounces his cock once in introduction. He drapes his arms up, in imitation of Samson, and launches himself, lazily, almost sultry, a Tennessee Williams heroine, down onto the tracks, and each step he takes causes his penis to pop upward. He looks ahead into the black, the Karen Black? Clint Black? The shirt comes up over his head, and is twirled into the plastic bag. He stops and gently moves his thumbs back and forth in his waistband. Smile. Down they went. White. Plump. A runner. He runs, walks, chugging rhythmically with his fist, and perhaps, *I have never felt so fully alive*. He thinks of this, hips brush the grains from a pipe, when do they say that? I have never felt so

... usually when they kill someone isn't it? Or after stealing a car ... he curls behind a pillar. The world is pathetic. A train crashes by and he freezes, but not completely. It comes to a stop, and from behind the pillar he can see light cast from a window directly behind him. Maybe someone is sitting there. Some tired old cleaning woman, coming home late, cleans offices after hours. He steps into the light, feels it bathe him and accelerates his masturbation, wanting to appear to her. A white form, a ghost, a chubby sexy ghost that haunts the subway. He has tried to time it so that he will come the moment she sees him. The car is empty and he lifts his hard cock up with two fingers, taunting, searching. The train lurches forward.

He walks behind it, pushing down on his cock. He's disappointed somehow. And seeing the platform loom once again, just ahead, he stops and turns. He feels the air soft against him, he thinks of a song, and he says his name, and it startles him, challenges him. Chastens him. Shames him, so he turns and—as if in defiance—begins to strut naked toward the platform. He's going to climb the steps, walk up naked, get arrested, so what? I'm not sick. If someone decides to approach you on the street, with his penis in his hand, is it necessary that he does this pathologically? Yes. He leans against you, you comfort him as his intensity passes, wipe your shoe, pat him lightly on the ass. A bright light, movie set bright. A train is coming, not coming, it's here. He folds in half and rolls under a ledge. The ledge recedes only a couple inches, and his entire body is hanging out, hovering in the headlights fifteen feet in front of the train.

A driver is seated at the front. He looks out, then bows his head toward the door, then back.

The third rail is inches away. Across a small space. *The light is so severe that my nipple casts a shadow up across his face. Penis tiny. Gone. Not a factor. Why won't the train move? Oh God. He can see me. The cops will come.* The plastic bag containing his clothes is behind his legs. *If I could get them on somehow, I could say I . . . what? I could say . . . I could pretend I'm drunk and . . .* He looks up and now there are two men in the driver's compartment. One guy'd just let you go maybe. Two guys beat the shit out of you. He pulls his knees up to free the bag. A sandal falls off, lands between the rails. A long black looping shadow. *Ok. Ok. I'm coming out. I'm in danger here anyway. I'm in trouble.* He rolls out, on his hands and knees, looking up at the front of the train. The two men, barely visible through the glare of light. *Are they looking? Can they see?* He takes out the shirt. No, shorts first. He lays on his side in the path of the train and pulls on his shorts. He stands, the shirt. He walks, head down, not sure if he isn't being watched the whole time, up onto the raised median, then along the side of the train. It appears empty. *What time is it?* He dashes across and vaults up onto the platform. *Made it! I did nothing here.* He walks quickly up the stairs. Exhilarated. The doors are locked. The subway is closed.

He walks back down slowly. A pay phone. He picks up the receiver and hits 0. Eventually he is speaking to transit security, who are a little miffed, but only a little, it's not that uncommon for them to have to fish people out of the system late at night. Drunks, passed out, kids fooling around sometime.

He hangs up the receiver. Wait. He picks up the receiver and dials an ex-girlfriend's number. After all, you can't tell this story to everyone.

VALID ALL ZONES

Jonathan Himsworth

Most of us had never seen a body on the rails before ... this one wasn't a corpse. It was alive. Obviously they had turned the current off and chased him like a fox from Embankment Station. He was blackened with the grime of the Underground, as if he had been rolling in coals and the absurdly white flecks of his eyes were the only contrast as he scampered out of the tunnel and onto the eastbound platform.

Most of us had never seen a cops-and-robbers chase either, and just as the police were about to catch up with him we got a four hundred foot fumbling example of it along the opposite deck. In pure style it took all three of London's finest to tackle and subdue the jammy rail-runner in a cloud of soot, ash and dust, confusing each other for the real thing. It had everybody riveted, and I for one was forgiving London Transport the disruption of service in lieu of the entertainment most of us patrons knew to be rare indeed.

Always a cheer for the perp. The only time I'd seen some-

thing similar was with a streaker at a football match, and automatically the crowd sides with the prey, wanting the chase to last as long as possible, egging on the bait, yaying when the cop stumbles.

A lot of deliberation was spent on how to bring the arrestee over to this side of the rails where the Transport Police office was. Eventually, after a prolonged wrestle, they managed to haul him up the stairs and around and wedge and budge him through the doorway of the small command post. A lot of bustle was centered on this little frosted door and there must have been a dozen officers contorting themselves before they were all inside, and the door shut.

The commotion had now subsided, and the general consensus was that the District Line had cleared the obstruction, and the train could now resume its course. I chose a thinly populated carriage, sitting across from two office ladies who I didn't take much notice of, and next to a man in an expensive suit towards whom I was soon to take more than a slight notice.

The doors remained patiently ajar, and I twitched beneath the exterior calm I had been projecting. I had faced delays before, but tonight was Election night, and I had yet to vote. An irritating chatter from the pair of office women managed to divert my agitation towards them. I wasn't much following their discourse, but had to look up when one of the women began pointing and warning the man next to me to take his feet off the seats. She was strictly in the right, but her attitude was immediately belligerent and offensive in itself. I for one, would have preferred her to leave off rather than make a meal of it, for the sake of the delay and the fact that by now everybody's day had been safely ruined. Who was to tell how many connections to planes, trains and dinners had been missed? Or votes. I wished she would just let the man relax and forget about it. She continued to nag like a neighbour with a grudge.

The man was a typical spiv. You see them only in London. They are the *nouveau riche* traders who have come from the ranks of the working class and "done good in the market." Many have come from families that traditionally traded fruit or scrap metal in the slums of the East End. They were good with numbers and able to substitute apples, oranges and corrugated iron off-cuts for yen and eurobonds. Now they could outclass even the Silver Spoons on the floors of the commodity exchanges and dealing floors of the City's finance houses in their bid to make, and show off, as much money as possible. The Silver Spoons are the privately educated Old Boys who were all rugby-playing chums in school and now help manage the funds of their elite friends. Two classes of capitalists side by side facing the same ocean of money. One reading the *Times* and collecting rare French artwork, the other reading the tabloids and watching football. The one thing in common to the two, is that they are almost always, invariably, unswervingly arrogant. It is a requisite for the industry. One will look down his aristocratic beak at you, and the other will snort down his common snout at you.

"Fuck off, you silly cow," summed up the spiv's essential sentiment towards our fellow passenger. The working class credo of always standing one's ground in a pub had come into play.

She feigned incredulity, as if she were a nun. Indignant and snappy, she yelped, "I beg your pardon?" as if she'd never heard a curse on a public train before.

"I said 'Fuck-off-you-silly-cow' so fuck off you silly cow and let me sit in peace." He made a bit of a leg stretch to show he had no intention of changing his posture, flumped his *Evening Standard* open to the betting pages and sighed wearily as if to say "some people!"

"How dare you!" she declared, beginning to create a storm. Her friend had joined in now and it was a double-barreled barrage of outrage at the man who had firstly, soiled the seat with his shoes, and now told them to fuck off, adding that they were cows.

He too now became heated and ready to match their level of aggro, and he stepped the abuse incrementally with each retort. I could no longer ignore this, or pretend to ignore this and I was now standing, joining in and saying "*Please*" really loudly. The two distressed women were boiling into an emotional frenzy, and in the flurry of jostling, the one who had kicked-off the complaining leant forward in an attempt to physically wrest the man's legs from their restful place. A confusion of arms, elbows and both male and female limbs twisted in front of me and suddenly she let out a loud gawp of panic to stun everybody.

"You bastard! You hit me! Violence against women you pig! Did you see that!"

"That's it," said her companion. "Enough! You've gone and hit my friend you beast!"

"Fuck off you silly cows."

I did not see anything that any of my sisters or brothers as five-year-olds would have considered a hit, and I think the woman was diving for a penalty, judging how absurdly she and her friend were now reacting.

"Citizen's arrest!" cried her cohort in a cat-like screech as she began taking him by the elbow.

"Let go of me you stupid woman!" growled the smartly dressed yob. The woman looked at me and asked, "You saw it! D'int ya? You saw it, right?"

I told her the whole thing seemed pretty ridiculous and I just wanted to get home quickly, get the vote in. I was ready to leave and run up to Fleet Street to get a bus. This was turning into a double bogey now so I stepped off the train and on to the platform just as the main victim scurried over to the Mickey Spillane door belonging to the British Transport Police.

The cockney yuppie was acting completely hard done by and saying he couldn't believe it. "Oh, leave it out," he kept imploring.

"You're under citizen's arrest for hitting my friend," kept reminding the other woman.

"Oh, f'fuck's sake shut it! The both of you. Awright?"

Meanwhile, with train still stationary, the victim was knocking on the glazed door and a gruff-looking cop peaked his head out. With little convincing he fully emerged along with a partner and they both stood there nodding and looking over towards our carriage, with the office door slightly ajar.

"You stupid fucking . . ." was the last thing I heard from the spiv's mouth. Out from behind the two nodding cops, jumped our favourite black sooty hedgehog rail runner, and in true dodge 'em turn-of-heel style, he sprang between the cops and legged it westbound down our side of the platform.

The two cops' duty to ascertain the woman's problem was immediately abandoned. They were joined by a faulty fire drill of ten other wobbly bobbies as they all bolted after the shaggy tunnel waggler.

That was it. Case closed. No human rights tribunal for the two women, and the spiv could now consign himself to another carriage. I watched half-interestedly as the comedy routine along the District Line resumed, and the gaggle of constables botched their way up the tunnel in the direction I wanted to go.

I ran up the stairs, saying to myself as I always . . . *Trust your instincts next time. You knew an idle train with its doors open was a bad sign.*

Getting up to Fleet Street, I was a panting wreck of lung-stung entrails and beery epiglottal stops, only to see a good ol' Routemaster heading for Victoria idling in traffic behind a cab twenty paces away. The open back door beckoned me as I ran down what hacks and tired editors once referred to as the Street of Shame. Chasing it, catching up to it, leaping, landing on my feet, surfing the platform as it skated beneath me and taking hold of the handrail, I finally surged with the torque of its mobility as the round red bus bounded forward, yanking me along in time for my first election.

THE COMMUTE

7:51 Tozai Line

Heather Watson

A wave of people
8 deep
And 6 wide
Leaning forward
Towards the doors,
Supported by bodies
As if
Suspended in gelatin,
Frozen in amber.
All wishing
For just this moment
To be Plasticine,
A Barbapapa,
And praying
That imminent
Decapitation
Will happen
To the person
Behind them instead.

Inside the train,
The standees,
All arms and legs
And giving flesh
Cupped to strangers
Thinly spread
Like cheese on crackers.
Outside,
The waiting throng
Presses hard,
And now disgorged,
I can look back,
Safer than Lot's wife.
In these tunnels
There are no apologies,
No rescue for the fallen.
Just thousands of
Lemmings,
Driven by the
Biological imperative
To get to work on time.
Dream on, young commuters.
The doors are inching shut,
And you are
Three salarymen back.

(*Tozai Line: a suburban subway line serving Tokyo)
(*Barbapapa: a shape-shifting cartoon character from the eponymous television show)

Pedestrian

Heather Watson

Unforgiving
Speed and motion,
Blurring shadows
Pavement's grit
Reaching up
To slap my feet,
So I strike first
In self-defense.
Slow my pace
And eat the dust
Of someone's gran,
A woolen shroud,
Rushing home
Another day
Of marking time
With *TV Guide*.
A slick of hair grease,
Tuesday's suit,
Contemplating
Fifteen years

A pimply son
Whose barbed-wire teeth
Save leftovers
From every meal.
And you,
My fallen glam-rock king,
Jeans tight as a
Blood-pressure cuff,
Self-important
In black leather,
Crushing bunnies
With each step,
A *carpet cleaner's*
Carpet cleaner,
AS IF I'd break
My stride for you.
Power poles,
Mailbox,
Telephone,
Crosswalk,
Get thee behind me,
Get thee behind me.
Yellow pardons,
Green invites,
My destination
Comes to me.
Speed and motion,
Show no mercy,
Take no prisoners,
Walk or die.

TWENTY YEARS OF
BLANK EXPRESSIONS

Matt Crisci

*A portrait of the brain-dead commuters one meets each
day traveling from suburbia to New York City*

The A.M. run for workaholics and the deeply insecure begins at six, if not earlier. The nine-to-five set board at eight, maybe later. But no matter the persona, the daily routine is exactly the same, always the same—grab an inky newspaper, pour a cup of acid-tasting black coffee laden with caffeine, no need to think so early in the day. About to enter the temple of non-cognitive thinking, the commuter train. A stainless steel barometric chamber, aseptically sealed, so nothing can germinate.

The platform oozes impatience, as 200 eyes, maybe more, dart rhythmically from clock to track, from track to clock. Impatience, in fact, is the food *du jour*. The train slowly screeches to a halt. To some, the noise pierces and penetrates an inner cavity. Others, so hardened by the routine, are totally oblivious. Each finely-tuned athlete is now limbering up at the starting gate. One last breath of fresh air, as it is. One last stretch of the slightly overweight and somewhat sedentary frame.

The train door bolts open. The starting gun sounds, the dash for the gold, silver and bronze begins. Gold for first preference seating in the front by the door; Silver, not bad aisle seats in the middle of the train. Still comfortable, not ideal. Bronze, the dreaded spot in the middle, where the arms of the passengers on the right and left subtly reside in your rib cage during the entire journey.

And what about those unfortunate enough not to win a medal? Those stoic warriors get to stand in the aisle by the exit door. Actually not so bad in summer, get a breath of fresh air now and then at the other stops. But in the winter, a blast of cold frosty air blows right up your ass!

With the first race over, all settle down, not a smile in the bunch. Newspapers scanned, laptops humming, a few random books being read. Bit of Salinger and Vonnegut, but mostly Krantz and Collins. Seated at eye level, you cannot help but notice the sea of newspapers held in hand with face behind. Imagine yourself sitting in the stands at a football game, the rooting section holding out placards, TV cameras directly in front recording the event for posterity.

If for no other reason than curiosity, I sometimes look back to see what's behind the placard, I mean the newspaper. What I see is what I expect, faceless blank expressions. It's so hard to accept that many of these blank expressions are the pillars of business and industry. Just for comic relief, I stare for a while. Not surprisingly, never once, not a glance acknowledged. Tiny immobile blue and brown irises, pupils, as if set in concrete retinas, stare straight ahead on both my left and right.

Aaah! There in the corner, some movement afoot. A well-groomed woman, in her early thirties, is applying her make-up, mirror in hand, bright lipstick being generously smeared from ear to ear. The train bounces on the track, the lipstick planned to highlight her mouth, instead lands definitively on her right cheek. No laugh here, just a painful moan and wistful sigh. A tissue to clean, a second application more determined than the first.

Further down the aisle sits a man and his bagel. Never time at home to eat before the daily journey to Urbanland, continental breakfast on the train instead. His muddy coffee resides in his personal stained cup, no need to use those Styrofoam cups, never know whose hands have been where. The cup just sits on the floor. Full before the train's bumpy ride began, the cup now splatters coffee here and there, like the slight belching of a smokestack in some steel-town factory. Can't help but notice other stains on the floor too, mostly juice, usually orange, hint of kiwi, touch of grape. And once in a while, blended Tropical Fruit, 90% sugar and water. Somehow gotta get that morning kick.

The one constant . . . the bagel. Solid and firm like a wrought-iron gate, impossible to break, spill or shake. Equally attractive with butter or cream cheese. Foolproof options, important for one trained not to have to think first thing in the morning.

Here comes Al the conductor, huge smile on his face. "Good Morning and Good Day." Not the slightest shift change in passenger expression. He continues anyway, just like the greeting had been returned.

In twenty years, Al has been the only one able to partially penetrate those blank concrete expressions. "Thank you for riding with us today," he continues with a passion. "I'd like to give you the weather report. Some clouds in the morning, chance of rain, maybe pick up an umbrella when you exit the train. Sunny by lunch time, so enjoy your meal. Crisp and clear this evening, perfect weather for the ride home and an after dinner walk with the family."

Finally, his warm and caring manner causes a break in the cold, dispassionate crowd. A few passengers actually look up. And one, the guy with the bagel in the corner, actually smiles and says "Thanks."

Al leaves, the blank expressions reappear. One thought on everybody's mind. *Within a short time we'll be at our destination. The ultimate coliseum, New York City. More specifically, the "Stadium of Manhattan."*

As we cross the last body of water at 138th in the South Bronx, a filthy puddle called the East River, I turn to view the city beachscape for a bit of refreshment. There I spot two guys in slumber, paper slipped from their hands, heads tilted to the side. The double-glass, hermetically sealed window, the lone barrier keeping these inanimate bodies from falling off the train into that muddy brown body of water.

As the train pulls into the platform, the scene changes. Expressions stay blank, of course. But, the working warriors are now suiting up for the daily joust. Ties tightened and fixed, jackets placed on like coats of armour. Women carefully squirming and wiggling to remove the wrinkles from clothing, checking their hair and makeup one last time.

The train waddles and screeches to a clumsy stop, as if to punctuate the reality, "We are here!" The train doors swing open. Hundreds of warriors bound from within. Imagine the Roman Coliseum when the gates opened and the Christians were thrown into the ring. The difference here, of course, nothing but blank expressions. Not one ounce of emotion in twenty years.

As the train empties, the last ritual even more startling. A guy in an $800 Hugo Boss suit, rummaging from seat to seat, looking for a twice folded, previously read 60-cent copy of the *New York Times*. "Ah, what luck today, a copy with nary a stain!" he says to himself.

Two last hurdles, then off to work we go. The first known as "atmospheric system shock." This phenomenon generally occurs when commuters leave the hermetically sealed train, air-conditioned to the perfect sixty-eight degrees Fahrenheit.

They spill into the dimly lit tunnel laden with fully exposed hot water and heat pipes that service the station above. The tunnel temperature on a good day? A comfortable ninety-four degrees with ninety-two percent humidity. And, not a sea breeze in sight.

The final hurdle, a drawbridge of sorts located at the end of the tunnel, just past the last passenger car. There stands a small exit, maybe four feet in diameter. All 300 or so now simultaneously attempt an exit. Each more impatient than the other. Sort of like the running of the bulls in Spain down neighbourhood streets. But there is a difference. That Spanish stampede is like a casual walk in the park compared to hundreds of upscale commuters each climbing over the other to enter the main terminal.

It's now six or seven or eight P.M.; the ritual reverses. First stop after entering that narrow gate, the barman with the rolling store. Just steps from the refuge of the air-conditioned train, a shot or two or three of legalized liquid Valium.

"Double Johnnie with a twist of lemon," utters the commuter warrior with the quivering hand. His perfectly neat morning uniform now in a somewhat lesser state. Hand outstretched to receive his Johnnie, his suit is wrinkled, shirt smudged, tie hanging loosely from his opened collar. The posture of a defeated man desperately needing the recharge of home.

Expressionless, they enter the train. A first refuge from the day's storm. But, in contrast to the morning, there is actually the sound of laughter and chatter. Our warriors are celebrating their survival through another day.

Upon leaving the tunnel known as Grand Central, the first thing one notices is the arrival of Harlem. Not quite the stereotype of many, but ghastly nonetheless. There, a red brick building so close to the train you could touch the mom and her children perched on the ledge of the rusty black wrought-iron fire escape.

To them their fire escape is like a view balcony, which allows them to take a pleasant respite from the dreary apartment just on the other side of the red brick wall. Listen closely, you can hear the thoughts of a few sensitive passengers that have noticed the family as the trains speeds by: *Despite how difficult things can be at times, I look at those people and realize how lucky I am to have what I have. I vow here and now to always live and breathe the glass as half full. Anything less I should be ashamed.*

The fact is, they will soon forget the promise made there and then. It is now halfway, the silence returns. The papers again raised as if to say "quiet please, time to prepare for family and friends." But in what seems like a matter of moments, the papers quickly slide into their laps. One by one, bobbing heads with droopy, heavy eyelids come to rest at the rear of their seats, closed mouths open. Looking down a row, one sees a line of baby bird mouths in slumber, waiting for mom to place a morsel of food in their open facial cavities.

The evening run is stocked with "regulars." Everybody tries to catch the same train every night, meet the same people. Meet in the bar car. It's kind of like one of those stuffy Clubs people spend so much to join.

But this day, the train is a bit more eclectic. Over in the right corner, sits a stray urban child, escaping the city with mom and dad, off to visit grandma and grandpa in the suburban countryside.

"Graaah!" roars the child, imitating a plane about to crash land. The child's sound, while not really that loud, reverberates in a train filled with silence. To open-mouthed patrons, eyes closed and heads to the rear, the *"Graaah"* sounds like the parting of the Red Sea, Moses and 20,000 Jews crossing.

This day a few other unusual sights. The man with tiny ear plugs and portable stereo player just across the way. Casual dress, gold chain on his arm, he pounds his feet, a gaggle of nerves. Seems a strange way to relax. Maybe that's why his expression remains so damn blank.

Directly across from "Gold Chains" resides a handsome man with an athletic physique. Maybe 6 feet 4 tall, sculpted muscle tone arms, not an ounce of fat. He is feverishly engaged in his hobby of choice—needlepoint. In his lap, he has designed the words "Home Sweet Home" in the shape of a heart. Looks like he's about seventy-five percent done.

A voice over the scratchy sound system reminds the patrons

aboard, "Last call for the bar car before we reach our first stop." The suggestion is obvious. Have one more *pop* to calm frazzled nerves. So when family and friends greet you at the station, you'll appear totally relaxed and calm for the evening ahead. One guy chuckles to himself "just gotta remember to chew some Dentyne gum, remove the odour of that last double Johnnie with lime."

Visiting the bar car, the difference from the rest quite clear. Patrons totally alert, so loud you can hardly hear when ordering a drink. Stocked with attractive types of the opposite sex, a bit like a bustling, noisy singles bar. But this bar is a bit different: it bounces up and down. It's like drinking on a trampoline.

Two carnivorous commuters surround a drop-dead blonde. Blackish blonde colour, killer dark eyebrows, a chin sculpted like Michangelo's David. Dressed in a flowing black dress, she could be spotted immediately in a room fifty times this size.

"So what do you do?" one bozo male patron asks. "I sell art in a gallery on 57th." The mating continues. She explains summer sales activity is slow, most of her usual patrons are in Cannes, Provence and the Hamptons.

"Not worried," she says, "I make up for it each fall. My regular customers return, make at least one purchase, seven figures or more. The commission alone allows me to live quite well."

She flirts with her eyes, as she continues. "In dead of winter, loaded with cash, I go where I please, choose who I want. Prefer to make the rules." Sensuous red lips darting around, teasing with the glass as she speaks.

Man number two, now secretly aroused, quietly removes his

wedding ring, not realizing the train is nearing his stop. *This is my living fantasy*, he thinks. *How can I be so lucky?* "Can I give you a ride home?" he suggests. "Go right by your place." "Thanks anyway," she says. "My husband is picking me up. Some other time perhaps."

The train comes to a halt; the ring quickly pulled from the pocket is returned to its rightful place. The doors open to a most pleasant scene. Moms and kids at the cars, some dads too. In this day and age, laying in wait for loved ones to appear. Smiles on everyone's face, as our warriors leave the train, they wave and smile. I imagine sort of like the soldiers who gaily returned home after World War II. The air so fresh and clean, the entire scene like a return to OZ. Not a blank expression in the crowd.

As each warrior enters the world of home, they take one last glance at the parting train. Conjuring a thought, inappropriate to share . . .

God, do I have to do that all over tomorrow? And tomorrow after that? For one fleeting instant, the blank expression returns. The one I've known these past twenty years.

MUSIC NOTE

Ryan Knighton

Imagine the girl
Collapsing to her seat.
Descending in scale
that #20 bus,
Musty in a spittle of rain,
Muggy in the summer
Shining. Her expression.

She rocks in its borrowed metal frame,
carried away,
& skittles, a party balloon
windy along gravel patches.

Legs unfold into the aisle & she
stretches bony
lyrical lines. Feet carried
in measured leather shoes.

It's a dream I have
dozing away home, waking
downtown startled.

Make the best
mistakes,

License to fetch our new favourites
from a store of hundreds.
Score second hand tunes,
this doggone day
chasing beauty in transit.

SPACE BETWEEN LIGHTNING AND THUNDER (BOWEN ISLAND)

Tammy Armstrong

I.
The Queen of Capilano waits
for the struggle:
foot passengers
with packs, cellulars, coffees
walk on, then up into the lounge,
5:45, a muffle of early morning voices,
those who will return at day's end.

My time here is finished,
the water no longer gilded,
     Chinese characters,
          floating
     waves beneath new risen sun.
This morning I stand on ferry deck,
ears protected from air horns as we pull away
into Howe Sound, away from the tourists,

the looky-loos who photograph the tavern,
cormorants still beneath loading dock.

I couldn't say goodbye,
couldn't get in that truck,
wait for the heat to kick on,
drive silently into the cove
with you still half-asleep.
My time here is through,
you are not the one
to keep the ferry from calling
to the mainland.

II.
Aubergine,
     hydrangea
this morning
a wreath of coastal mountains—
scar tissue
the frost-crusted ferry moves easily through.

With you hilled in some cabin,
I took to bird-watching
the bluejays and blackcapped warblers
who argued on spruce trees—
blue and black as a summer evening
children raced on bicycles to beat;
while the screeches grew,
daylight tangled in the whining spokes
and the wings of night reclaimed
their slope of land.

III
Your need always on the side of stone—
circumstance,
involuntary moments when we remembered
an isolation
your whelk-shaped thoughts could bear,
but Vancouver—
    sin city beneath wind cripple
called out street corners, life,
an extension of imagination, familiarity.

This past year,
I worried too much
about cutting my fingers with bread knives.
The bloodstone path from kitchen to backyard
where I would stop—hand cupped in hand—
realising there is nothing
but rusted axe, hunting fridge
and you, now as you are,
reading the newspaper
over your first cup of coffee
    while commuters wait for passage
    deep in Snug Cove.

IV.
One hundred miles
    beneath a pullet angry sky,
from ferry to Horseshoe Bay
    a streak along the coast
until I'm swallowed up
into Central Station Greyhound—

an ever accelerating constellation
    sprinting me home.

But for now leaning over the bulwark,
cigarette smoke trails thin,
propellers churn,
    we pull away from the dock.
Bowen Island shrinking,
finally into small mound of trees,
    winged water near the marina—
        vitreous,
a small distance to mean so much.

STRANGE RIDES

BLOOD TRANSFER

Gregory Betts

I was wasted and my nose was bloody. I wasn't wasted *because* of the blood, though it had been many years since my face had been so runny, and the pain of a broken nose was confused with my feeling of self-consciousness. I had refused to use the sleeves of a new shirt, or my hands, to wipe away the blood. Each nostril was plugged with subway transfers. The front of my shirt was speckled red, anyways, but that didn't change anything. I can be a real stubborn bastard when I'm drunk.

Behind me, as I walked, I left a long trail of white silence. People moved away from me, even as they were drawn and pulled in, peeling away details for their own misbegotten pleasure. Even the last subway, usually a testament to the merry, bold, and bizarre souls of Toronto, eyed me askance for my face and body. They stared because I was disgusting. And because I was so wasted that I didn't care, sat smoking openly in the subway car, in front of fifty eyes, and coughed.

And let the blood bleed through crinkled transfers. Nobody sat next to me so I threw my legs up on the seat and pretended to pass out.

I waited on the ground of the bus platform alone and smoked. Eventually the all-nighter that rolled near my house ambled in, and the driver got out and stood above me and lit a cigarette. He didn't hide his curiosity, just smoked and got his fix of gore for the night. I wanted to ask him if he liked David Cronenberg, but my tongue wouldn't respond. We just smoked and looked at each other until he motioned to the no-smoking sign above my head.

"Don't fine me, eh?"

When I tried to chuckle, the first flood of pain hit me. I doubled over, embarrassed and crotchety. But he came over and half-dragged me on my ass into the bus. He left me on the top step, with a still burning cigarette, and the door wide open. I noticed, but only half-believed, that he was still smoking, himself, as we pulled out of the station onto York Mills Road. I watched the sidewalk stream by through the open door, thinking that he hadn't asked me for a transfer.

"Which way you going?" he asked.

He stopped in front of my house when I told him, and we sat there for a minute while I finished my cigarette. I couldn't talk, I was holding back sobs with my everything, but I wanted to thank him. I turned and tried to burn some message into his mind with my eyes, but he was only looking at my bloodied face. I got off and watched him roll down my little suburban side-street, turn at the first chance, and disappear back onto a lonely late-night beat, probably amused by curiosities. I stopped thinking, wiped my face with my sleeve, and pulled out two rich red transfers from my nose.

My Empty Sleeve

Mark Anthony Jarman

Generations are split, I note, by eyewear, weight, and where they sit on the #11. Your mileage may vary. Our bus driver motors happily past the neo-Brutalist brick fortress; she motors straight past the corner where we are meant to turn right, turn away every twenty minutes from the hook of the frozen sea.

Our driver laughs at herself, says with a French accent, Guess I was supposed to hang a right back there.

I imagine myself stranded and cursing at a stop on that lost stretch: Did I miss the bus again! Why does this always happen to me!? No idea *why*.

We breeze through a neighbourhood where golden retrievers are walked in eager unison, rich quiet houses with scented dryers on tumble and no worries about why, confident their taupe eggs are not all in one basket.

The fortress home where our driver failed to turn: *every brick, every brick felt a hand.*

Hey. Is this the 14?
Two young ballcaps at the door.
We're waiting for the 14.
This is the 11. Only the 11 on this route.
We'll wait for it.
They sit down at the stop.
Driver says, I am the 11.
You are? Not 14?
I am the 11.
Oh.

They climb up sheepish and angry because they're not from a ghetto. By not being deprived, they've been deprived. O to be born in a ghetto, to get jiggy with the rats and rasta players.

We cut toward town, a brain in every eye. Passengers look preoccupied, working on their theory, their idea for a new flavour of ice cream: *Fishsticks On The Moon?!*

Like Doubting Thomas I touch the yellow pole, jump off by the gas-lit steakhouse. Orestes is at the Cineplex. Downtown they are barking, breaking the statues, one memory hitting the others like a pool ball *(You break)*.

Inside the steakhouse the man named Leckie says, You want to work?
What hours?
Full-time. Work hard?
Yeah sure. What hours?
Full-time. Work hard?
Pause.
Well, yeah, okay.

Leckie touches his speed-dial phone, bellows into it: WES I GOT YOUR PERMISSION TO HIRE A DISHPIG? WES I COME IN

AND IT'S A FUGGIN MESS, NO ONE "FUGGIN" CLEANS UP!

Customers stare from their steak and lettuce and garlic tinfoil.

GOTTA SORT OUT "FUGGIN" FORKS AND KNIVES, IT'S A FUGGIN MESS, CRACKERS EVERYWHERE, NO ONE FOLDED ANY NAPKINS.

I CAN'T HIRE HIM I WALK.

IT'S A FUGGIN MESS.

OKAY WES YOU BETTER GET OVER HERE AND DO DISHES CUZ I'M FUGGING WALKIN.

OKAY WES I'M WALKING!

Leckie leaves, he's walking, it's not a bluff.

Sue the waitress apologises to a pretty woman on a business trip. "Sorry, don't know what's with him today." Sue gives the businesswoman seven hot sauces and does her Texas waitress imitation: *This one so hot it'll make you slap yo mama!*

Sue the waitress touches a blue screen, and FUCK! echoes from hidden kitchen, fry cook runs out in flames. The waitress calmly sprays him down, sprays his white smock and black eyeglasses.

I'll just leave my application on file, okay? I say to no one. Thanks! I say to no one. I walk into the snow, walk where the other guy just 'walked.' Days of snowstorms, no sidewalk for freezing weeks and you miss the harvest moon's warm grin, the moon's prepared talk: *Hello son.*

A little snowsuit kid tethered to a tree, four or five, about the age of my youngest, and this kid looks at me and says, "In my world I'm twenty-one!"

In my world I'm about ninety, in my world I need a drink or two.

Bartender says fast, *Jerry Who's Jerry? Jerry-atric?*

The Florida Panthers: backcheck, stick, elbow, trip, slew-foot, pitchfork, spear to groin—whistle, whistle, whistle. Try Enigma Beer, says the coaster: You're never sure what it tastes like.

A man dabbling in double ryes says to me, "You know that old Eskimo chief on the $2 bill, hell you know him, well he got killed dead going over a cliff in a snowmobile. Now if that's not a metaphor," he says, "if that's not a metaphor . . ."

We're paying extra to see gilded breasts, pay them to rise off the ribs, we want that breast to be a beautiful eye that turns and sees something special in us. I'm downtown with the pariahs—isn't this what I crave? Golden naked ghosts in go-go boots, sleet in white lines like fibre optics, and more Liebensbraum than you can possibly handle.

I rush to the bus stop, worrying I have Prog-Rock tendencies, jump on the #11 once more. It goes the wrong way, circles around the zoo, the Hotel-Dieu Hospital, the Rebel Motel. I forgot they changed the routes again. They change them every week or two to keep us on our toes. Drive here, drive there, turn left, turn right—soon I'm the only seasick passenger left.

The driver is short with long blonde hair. She stops the bus. She yells something.

I'm way at the back, about a mile back.

What?

Sir, where are you getting off?

Oceanside ends the ride. The mysteries of Hicksville.

What!?

I walk up to the front so we don't have to yell, so we can be civilized.

She says, You should have gotten on the bus at Smut Tek. You know, by Tuna Pizza. That's the new stop. There were a couple tiny signs that the wind has probably blown down by now.

Signs?

Signs. At the old stop by Eaton's.

Eaton's?

I could make you get off, I could charge you twice. I have eight minutes here for my coffee break. This is my break. It belongs to me. Do you have people hanging around on your coffee breaks?

I don't drink coffee. What is wrong with this picture? There I am at the back reading a newspaper and you yell so I walk up to the front and then you berate me for hanging around on your break. I'm not *hanging around*. Do you think my idea of big fun is watching you drink coffee for eight minutes? I'm trying to get *home*. This is my bus, the 11.

But this isn't the Oceanside 11, this is the Zooside 11. I could make you get off.

Is there the teensiest chance you and management could work this out on your own?

Sir, you're breathing alcohol on me.

I stomp back to my newspaper and we stew for eight minutes. Devotion comes with age but the wrong devotion. I am an animal with a product code and I have ruined her break. Lamp globes inside the zoo are lit blood oranges and the elephant is insane. This is not far from where they caught the bumbling smack-head bank robbers. I wish I was shooting skeet at Bill's farm. Five-4-3-2-1: the bus finally roars to life and glad of it we are. Other riders climb on, but the blonde driver and I have our secrets.

A big woman trots on board by the mental hospital. Hi, how are you today? She asks me in a very happy voice.

Pretty good, I lie, wondering if I have a sign on me or something.

Cold out tonight, I got a coffee at Starbuck's. I got a new job at the hospital gift shop. Here's a nice girl, here's a nice girl. Hi girlie! How are you?! Eggs on today at Safeway, $1.64 a dozen, one per customer, not a bad price, bye!

She rides one block to buy a coffee and rides one block back. She rides back and forth. We're pale passengers rejected from some vague contest or charm school, yes we've lost some close elections.

Then we're on a country highway, we're by pine woodlots on a salmon river, and a smell wracks us from the feed plant on Vanier Avenue. I seem to have traveled from BC's restless army of addicts to New Brunswick river towns—a changeling country.

The bus pulls over by a shingle cabin with many lean-tos hammered to the original and a moose in a corral. I can see in the lit cabin windows. A mother and children have baked blackbirds in a pie.

What the hey? Wonders the blonde driver at a map, must've missed something back there somewhere. Keep changing these darn routes!

And the area code, says a passenger, they changed our phone's area code!

After VE Day a lone U-boat refused to surrender, snuck out of the Baltic Sea, and crossed the Atlantic to South America, last of the Reich's wolf packs. Took them a long time, underwater most of the time, afraid to be spotted by Allied planes or destroyers. No sunlight, no fresh oxygen, the U-boats's air poisoned by the mammoth batteries, everyone coughing in bunks and everything drips water, pipes and bulkheads and sausage covered with mildew, no ersatz coffee, bread wet and moldy, the sailors' skin gone weird haunted colours—an invisible crew caught between bottom and top.

We're trapped inside that U-boat, and I'll never see home again. Our faces are starting to look like the pictures jailed on our driver's license.

Inside the shingled cabin three boys chase each other with pistols that are actually a yellow hose nozzle, a piece of wood, and a red bicycle pump.

Bang bang! Kioo! Kioo!

The eight-year-old boy shoots the four-year-old boy and the younger boy falls.

The U-boat pipes are dripping, wrapped like a boxer's hand.

"You want to come put away some laundry?" a pretty mother asks. She stands by the bed wearing soft PJ bottoms warm from the dryer, wears nothing else.

"No thank you," says the younger child pleasantly. "Right now I'm dead."

Detached: on the #148 to Ioco

Carla Elm

I'm feeling detached like a retina
at the back of eyes beaten and bruised.
My vision is out of focus
leaving me to imagine
body language.
I ride my bus past the place where she was
grabbed by her hair or backpack
beaten unrecognizable
teeth shattered
fists and
feet pounding
into shocked flesh
sending cries inaudible
over grunts of
mother
fucker.
Blood oozed to a point
beneath hatred weight bent

flesh wrapper tossed
on concrete to lie
like garbage until morning
waiting for their stops.
I look sideways into a stranger's eyes
hold my transfer in my hand,
ready to run
for my connection,
rising in my head
without emotion
the childhood jingle:
*'Someday my Prince will come,
chewing Wrigley's spearmint gum.'*

For Calvin Wharton

NOTE:
This poem was inspired by a violent event that happened across from an apartment block in which I used to live in Coquitlam, B.C. A young Polish woman walking home at two in the morning during the summer of 1995 was attacked and beaten to death. Her assailant remains unknown to this day.

RETARD

Grant Buday

Everything about him said one thing—retard. His wet-lipped gaze, his hands stuck to his thighs, the way he sat still as a stump. And he was next to the only empty seat on the bus.

It was August. Sunday. Hot. More people squeezed on. That seat stayed empty. No one wanted to sit next to a retard, especially a big one. You gotta be careful around the big ones 'cause they're strong. When I worked in the mental hospital there was a retard named Conrad. Every morning he made me sit on his back while he did push-ups. He could do thirty-five push-ups with me on his back. I'd sit there going up and down up and down, keeping count for him.

Everyone on the bus was sweating. The retard wasn't, even though he wore a yellow ski jacket zipped to his throat. Maybe it was his meds. You could feel people eyeing that seat and deciding no way. You'd be trapped between him and the window. He'd have you prisoner. What if there was an accident?

Or some immigrant with a gun started shooting? You'd never get out. And even if nothing went wrong, you'd have to breathe his air, air that had been in his lungs. Like most retards, he breathed through his mouth. At the hospital I heard how Mongoloids have such long tongues they can stick them up their own noses.

No one took the seat. The guy kept offering it, though. He was polite. At every stop he said, "Free seat, please, free seat."

Old ladies lugging four bags of groceries pretended not to hear. A pregnant woman lied and said "I'm only going one stop." People ignored him, made like they were fascinated by the ads. *Read The Province. Cheques Cashed. Chew Trident.* Helene would have sat down next to him no problem. That's how she was. Every time new people got on, the retard swung his legs into the aisle like he was opening a gate. "Free seat, please, free seat." He had a monotone voice, like a recording, and he didn't get insulted when no one wanted to sit by him. He was too dumb. He just swung his feet back in, put his hands on his thighs, and stared ahead as if the windshield was a TV. His hands looked like albino starfish stuck to his legs.

I was on my way home from visiting my friend Edward. He'd had a stroke. I always thought what a weird word that was: stroke. I mean, you stroke a cat, you stroke your dick, the guy at the back of the canoe shouts *Stroke! Stroke!* through a megaphone. Heart attack made more sense. But Edward told me a stroke was worse than a heart attack. His whole right side was paralyzed. He laughed and said he was now a southpaw. That was another one I never understood: southpaw. It's like it means people always stand with their right arm to the north and left to the south. I don't know. I saw a show on left-handed people. There are proportionately twice as many lefties in jail than right-handed people. Plus they die younger because of accidents, and they're more likely to be queer. Leonardo da Vinci and Michelangelo were both left-handed queers. I learned that on PBS. Helene liked PBS.

The bus wobbled its way along Hastings Street, past that Pink Pearl dim sum place, then the Glenhaven Memorial Chapel. That's where Helene's Uncle Victor died. Went in to arrange his mother's funeral, heard the price, and had a heart attack. Keeled over and hit his head on a coffin.

My hand was going numb from gripping the pole. Whenever I have to hold onto the pole I always hunt for a cool spot where no one's been touching it, because people's hands teem with bacteria. That's the word the guy on TV used: teem. He was a biologist. He said there's more bacteria on your palm than in your mouth. So doing mouth-to-mouth is cleaner than licking someone's hand.

Before leaving the hospital today I went to the can and scrubbed my hands with soap and water. It was because Edward shook my hand when I arrived, shook it again when I left, and all during the visit covered his mouth with that same hand and coughed into it.

We turned right onto Commercial Drive and the bus's rods dropped from the overhead power lines. Everyone groaned except the retard. He just sat there like he didn't mind, looking straight ahead at the windshield like he was watching cartoons. People walking past looked in at us. I remember how at the hospital, some guys all they did was walk up and down the hall. Psychiatrists say walking relaxes retards and crazy people. Something about the motion. We walked them in the mornings and we walked them in the evenings, like they were dogs. Other than that they watched TV. The driver couldn't get the rods hooked up and everyone started getting antsy. The guy standing in front of me had a bald spot shaved in his hair, and stitches. I counted seven stitches. It was like Frankenstein. I looked at the ads. *Cancer Can Be Beaten. Make a Will. Visit Cuba.* Helene always wanted to go to Cuba.

The driver climbed back in and everyone felt relieved. We ploughed our way up Commercial to Broadway, where a blind woman got on.

It's hard not to stare at a blind person. It's like when someone's asleep, you get to watch without being watched back. The blind woman didn't wear glasses, and her eyelids looked like warts. The retard said, "Free seat, please, free seat." We all watched the old lady follow his voice, her hand moving from one seat back to the next, her white cane tapping the rubber floor like the feeler of some big bug. She slipped past the retard's knees without even touching him. Like she was only faking being blind. She arranged her purse and her cane, then turned her head to the right as if she was looking out the window. A blind woman.

Lately they've been rerunning that show about the blind detective. I wonder what it'd be like to watch blind people hump. Or retards. Some show I saw said retards are horny. I wonder what it'd be like to be blind, left-handed, retarded and queer. Sometimes I think Edward is queer. He asked how Helene was.

The last time I saw Helene we were finalizing the divorce. She'd lost sixty-three pounds and was getting remarried—get this—to a Moroccan named Iqbal. I warned her about Moroccans. I told her how I'd seen a show about them. She got pissed off and said I was prejudiced. The show said Moroccans had different attitudes about women. They interviewed some Irish woman who'd married a Moroccan and had to smuggle herself out of the country in a shipping container because she was a prisoner in the house. And even when she did get to go out she had to have a chaperone and wear a veil. They showed a street scene in Morocco. The women looked like beekeepers. I told Helene to be careful, and I confess that even though we were washed up I still loved her. At Kingsway a bunch of people got off the bus. Then at 33rd I got a seat, one of the singles on the left side. Those are the best. You don't get stuck next to anyone. By 41st the bus was almost empty and I started to relax.

Despite the divorce, I was thinking who knows, maybe me and Helene still had a chance. People change. That's what they said on this show. People change. The show said that without the belief in change we'd be reduced to Asiatic standards of fatefulness and apathy. Those were the words, fatefulness and apathy. It was our belief in self-improvement that made the West superior. Besides telling Helene be careful, I told her I'd changed. I said how I'd been developing an appreciation for *Jeopardy*, answering the questions and everything, because it's good when two people in love love the same show. It's good. It's something to share.

By the time we hit 49th and the top of the hill, it was just me, the blind lady and the retard, all staring out that window, and you know, it was kind of nice. I figured that ride could just go on and on, because moving like that was soothing, you relaxed, you forgot yourself.

GIFTS

M.A.C. Farrant

I called for an early morning taxi and they sent a hearse. In a cunning effort to keep my mood black, I reasoned. A hearse. Making sure I got the point. But I got in. Liking the way the hearse idled in the driveway like a limousine. The way the uniformed driver opened the door, solicitous as an usher. Inside the hearse: music playing—Mozart's *Requiem* or it could have been *Pink Floyd At Condo Hall*. I sat in the front seat beside the driver feeling strangely buoyed: we were carrying no casket.

Traveling to the city, then, at a funereal pace. Noting the sober glances from passersby: a woman at an intersection with a look of heavy concern; a group of pensioners staring grimly. I smiled and waved, determined to be sunny.

Delivered at length to Forty-Fifth and Sharpe. There to walk the streets, my pockets full of dollar coins. To dispense at random to the squatting street kids with their dogs, sleeping bags, packs. And when a man asked for a cigarette I gave him the one I was smoking. And when a drunk holding an empty Listerine bottle said, "Spare change?" I gave him the rest of my coins. Thinking: whatever happened to Karl Marx?

Thinking: gifts. And the pigskin wallet that you in your downy life might possibly need. Visiting the warehouse where my old friend Mona practiced supply side economics. In theory. Seven hundred pigs and a staff of twelve. The staff toiling third world fashion—strip, snip, toss. With a conveyer belt to the Chinese restaurant next door. The warehouse air chemically treated—made cool and sweet—keeping the pig skins supple. Row upon row of skins hanging from lines like laundry.

And last week in the mail from the Bank of Commerce, another gift: Free Accidental Death Insurance to the tune of fifteen hundred dollars. For being a loyal consumer.

What is this business of giving?

Choosing your wallet from the many pig skin items happily displayed. Buying wholesale. Thinking dear. Thinking: business might be a good way to go: simple rules and your nose aquiver with ad campaigns, market forces: your life reduced to yea or nay. And Mona to admire, a woman meaning business, with advice to give: *Oppose takeover bids. Prune your life of all things grey—sluggish partners and so forth.*

And will you admire your new wallet with its pouches greedy for your extra bills? Bought with wholesale intentions, mainly dear, love and so forth. And will my gift prove to be a wise investment? Thinking: what ever happened to Walt Whitman, that freewheeling champion of giddy days?

Propelling myself, then, to the afternoon reception where I paid homage to three floors of newly installed books.

Keeping my mood on the far side of black. In theory. So many books. So little interest. Helped along in this endeavour by complimentary wine and sushi. Prowling the guests for advantage. And meeting Karen entertaining a crowd about Jack: *I got him straight from his mother and she practically wiped his ass. He doesn't know what helping is. Comes home, sits in front of the TV, plays with his computer. Gives me a face if I ask him to feed the dogs.*

Thinking: whatever happened to the Dalai Lama and the untainted, generous life?

Back on the streets. The sun shining in spite of itself. A city duly warmed. Imagining the pile-lined slippers I might possibly buy. Another gift. For your nightly, TV vigil. Compounding my investment; my mood surging to bright. And will your feet in pile-lined slippers thank me, thank me? Your feet tender from years of giving your all: pounding pavements, carpets, linoleum, grass.

Meeting my friend Heather, then, for coffee at five dollars a pop. Coffee in theory. Made with chocolate, whipped cream, ad campaigns. The conversation turning to her lover, Ross: *They don't understand, do they? They don't consider* COMPLEXITY. *For them it's all business, the bottom line.*

Uh huh.

Thinking: intravenous Buddhism. Cleverly attached to our sleeping arms—subliminal brain-washing pumping us full of kindness, wisdom, love. And will the man asleep in the pet shop doorway thank me, thank me?

Thinking of what Sarte said: There are two ways to go to the gas chamber, free or not free.

Entering, then, the waiting hearse for my return trip home. Our newest form of public transportation, tailor made for those of us preferring the slow, gloomy sweep, the funereal glide. The hearse taking me home. Where I'm a volunteer participant in whatever falls my way. Sometimes smiling, sometimes not.

And yesterday by mail a blessing from St. Mary's Church. With a special message from the church wardens: *Please, we need your money.*

Giving and taking. Thinking: our ability to reconcile dark with light has diminished.

Filling out my coupon for a bag of microwave popcorn. Free with a fill-up at Save-On-Gas.

Intent on having giddiness, too.

HAVE YOU EVER BEEN TO THE PA BUS STATION?

Betsy Trumpener

Everyone with broken bones was traveling north with you on the STC bus from Saskatoon. Small boys coming home from hospital, curling the good arm against their mothers. And the men were not drifters. They had babies in their hands. Or they carried long tubes of plans for northern minerals and rocks. Or they were biologists, smelling of deep woods and moss beds. They penciled little notes in their fieldbooks as we rode:

— Sarsaparilla: woodland herb — historically treated VD — now, makes root beer

— Core Sample Volume values

— Today, felt 100g of fear . . .

— To milk a bison, first you must truss it up something fierce.

Like this we traveled, with only a short stop in Rosthern. Drove right past the site of the Duck Lake massacre.

In Prince Albert, an old woman was calling to me across the terminal. I could barely see her, waving urgently at me with her body hid behind the bathroom door.

— Me? Who me?

I have a thing about bus station bathrooms. I really prefer to use the back of the bus. I don't like to see travelers from Ontario bathing their armpits in the sink. More, it's this, that when you swing open a stall door, you never know what you will find.

This old woman, though, it was nothing like that. She had a broken wrist still swelling in its cast. Arm in a sling on the way to the first cousins' funeral past La Ronge. Five dead this year already, she tells me. Her daughter comes by in the morning to tie up her shoes.

— If you could braid my hair, she says. Can do nothing for myself now. Not tight, she tells me. Just nice. Her hair is very long and black and thin and I split it in three and then I bring it all back together. I want to say: Thank you for asking.

I light her a smoke, taking the first draw for myself and pack the fruit back into her bag from the washroom counter. And I find her pain pills. —Take some, go ahead, she tells me.—It's good for that hard piece of pain. And then I sit outside on the dried piss stains of the PA bus station and nothing happens. Nothing at all.

LOVE ON A STREETCAR

Marion Lydbrooke

Gita hadn't wanted sex since the cat died. Then on the streetcar Martha saw Zoe, the electrician from Pope Joan's. Zoe was all wet from the summer rain, in tight jeans and punky fuschia hair, an untouchable mutant sea-creature licking Martha from her horny shell where she itched and grated. Like when Gita tied her to the bed as they held their breath to stop from coming, making it go on like they were riding a track forever.

At Spadina, Zoe squished onto the seat beside her and said, Hi. Oh hi, said Martha, combing her tatty hair with her hand. Zoe's skin was smooth as butter. Martha wondered, ten years younger than me? Six, maybe? Is she in love with that leather girl she always dances with?

By Peter Street they hadn't said much. Shyness perhaps. Martha was curious to know where Zoe was off to but didn't ask. She could smell a trace of mango on Zoe's drenched hair, could feel Zoe's muscled thighs against hers, tried not to gape at her hard melon breasts. But by John Street Martha was dying of lust. Close your eyes and think of England, her aunt used to say when Martha was little, squirming under the jolly dentist's knobbly fingers exploring her mouth.

At John, she started deep breathing into the backs of passengers hanging on in front of them, rocking and swaying like drunken marionettes to the rhythm on the track. *Itchy itchy slippery wet itchy itchy slippery wet.* By McCaul, Martha was babbling to herself. *Zoe's way too young for me, way too young! And Gita said she'd leave if I cheated, even once.*

The streetcar was sweltering once the rain let up. Between York and Yonge Martha was desperate for everyone to get out and give her some relief. By University, with Zoe still firmly against her, Martha decided not to go to Pope Joan's anymore, not to go anywhere near Zoe, or any clubs where she'd likely be. Gita would soon get over the cat dying. Anyway, so what if they never had sex again? Martha loved Gita's intense, brainy, soft, fat, dark-haired, witty peculiarities. Gita just got a kick out of saying no. It was a game they played. Gita knew it turned Martha on, making her agitated and restless.

At Yonge, people got out and more climbed on, bringing a slight breeze and the smell of damp clothes. The sun slickered through the window, still dripping from the rain. Zoe turned to Martha and said, Got another cat, yet?

Not yet, said Martha. Gita's still upset. She tried controlling her voice to hide the lust in her throat, imagining Zoe's forbidden silky breasts brushing against her. *No, you can't come.* Gita loved to say over and over, enjoying Martha's increasing frenzy.

The streetcar jerked and Zoe jostled into her. Martha took a sharp breath, held it. Zoe's fingers had somehow found their way onto Martha's shoulder, wiring Martha's nerves. The car jolted again. Martha turned and her eyelash twitched as they locked eyes. Zoe's smell danced in Martha's nose. Martha's mouth was dry, the air like treacle.

I like you, whispered Zoe. Pity I'm spoken for. Zoe licked her finger like it was chocolate, slipping it between Martha's lips as Martha closed her eyes and gently, slowly, sucked it. She opened her eyes slowly to find Gita staring at them. Martha went cold, then hot. Zoe, catching on, calmly slithered her finger out, stood up, said goodbye, slipped between the marionette passengers and disappeared.

You're a bitch, Gita hissed to Martha. I knew something was up between you two. We're finished! The marionettes gawped as Gita stomped down the steps, the doors clattering shut behind her. Wait! Cried Martha, but Gita was gone and the streetcar was lurching forward again. Martha closed her eyes to the twirling patterns behind her lids and murmured, *Fuck. Fuck. Fuck.*

As they rattled towards Broadview, Zoe's finger-spice was still dancing on her tongue. The streetcar was nearly empty now. She forgot where she was going, didn't care. All she could hear was the streetcar rattle and her aunt's dirty laughter and remembered the dentist's knobbly fingers pressing against the soreness of her gums.

Let Your Fingers Do the Walking on the #9 Broadway

Bonnie Bowman

I'm on Broadway, but there's nothing dramatic about it. This ain't New York, after all, this is Vancouver. It happens to be one of those interchangeable weekdays and I'm waiting at the Willow Street bus stop for the #9 Broadway, heading east. The time is afternoon rush hour, and the weather surprisingly hot for this city. Having just finished a shift at Vancouver General Hospital, I wait with several other hospital workers, all of us in our uniforms and white sneakers, smoking cigarettes, none of us personally acquainted. I will be taking this bus to Broadway and Commercial Drive, and all I care about is getting a seat.

The sun is hurting my eyes and my rumpled white uniform dress is sticking to the backs of my bare legs. I probably have a hangover, but this is all occurring in the late '80s so now I'm guessing. My arms are clutching a stack of binders and folders and, please God, don't make me have to stand. That's all I'm thinking. And really, that's your only concern at this time of day. If you're taking a bus at three in the morning from Main and Hastings, you have other concerns. You expect drama. You're prepared for anything. But not in afternoon rush hour.

The bus heaves into the stop, followed closely by another number nine, and the uniforms troop single-file into the second bus, relieved. I get a seat, a double seat, window. Hugging my folders to my chest, I hunch myself towards the window and lean my head against the grime, closing my eyes. At the next stop, someone sits beside me. I don't look over, don't even flinch. Whoever it is has perfected appropriate seat etiquette and is not intruding on my space. Were it not for a faint scent of aftershave, or cologne, I wouldn't even know someone was there.

I dream. I am running barefoot through a sparse forest, light on my feet, sailing over rocks and logs and pools of swampy water. A man is chasing me, a soldier type man who is wearing a bandana on his head and a rifle slung across one shoulder. He is lean but muscular, dark-complexioned, and his boots thud on the forest floor as he closes the distance between us. I am laughing, my hair streams out behind me. I soar effortlessly through the trees and birds fly up before me, startled, screeching. The soldier is getting closer, I can hear his breathing now, quick, ragged, insistent. I breathe freely, cleanly, embrace the sweet air—I am a dancer. As I turn my head back to look for the soldier, my toe catches a branch. I am falling, lightly, breathlessly, and collapse in a heap of skirt and leaves and twigs. The soldier catches up and stands over me. His breathing is quick, harsh, and louder now. There is no other sound. I open my eyes a slit and look up at him, his face in shadow, lit from behind by the sun. I believe he is going to rape me. But it's one of those cool rape fantasies where the rapist is really good looking and you're into it. I pretend to be unconscious, squinting at him through my hair, waiting for him to do something. And then I feel it. His rifle barrel on my leg, slowly moving up, lifting my petticoats with it.

Then something happens. My conscious brain kicks in. Droning bus sounds filter into the dream, and I struggle to recapture the fantasy. Until I realize ... there really is something on my leg, just above my right knee. And it's moving up. Holy shit, I'm awake now. But I don't panic, I wait until I'm fully aware of my surroundings and assess the situation.

At first I think my seatmate is holding an umbrella or something and it's fallen against my leg. Okay. But it's the middle of summer and this 'umbrella' is definitely making a slow and inexorable progress up my thigh. I open my eyes a slit and without moving my head, swivel my gaze down and to the extreme right. This exercise hurts my eyes and skews my contact lenses. But I do manage to see it's not an umbrella. It's a hand. More specifically, the index finger of a hand. And it's ever so slowly inching up my leg towards the hem of my dress. My first thought is ... *what the fuck?* But I make no move, I can't believe the boldness of it. Does this guy think I'm asleep? It only takes a few seconds but I think of a hundred different actions I could take, most of which would cause severe physical pain. A sharp jab of my elbow to his side. A quick backhanded fist to the bridge of his nose. Slam my heavy binder down on his knuckles and crush them. Or just say something really, really loud and embarrass the shit out of him.

But for some reason, I don't do any of these things. Instead, I'm wondering who he is. Gotta be some pervert, I'm thinking. Maybe a dirty old man, pathetic, or perhaps someone with a mental illness, pitiable. So here's what I do. Without looking at him, without moving, I just say, very quietly: "What do you think you're doing?"

The finger stops. Silence. Then his voice, also very quiet. "Don't you like it?"

What? I can't believe it. Of all the possible responses, I didn't expect that one. This is when I open my eyes and slowly turn my head to look at him. I'm ready to lay into this creep, whose hand still sits benignly on my leg. And there he is, looking all of thirteen or fourteen years old. Shit, he could even be twelve. And he's not some weird little punk with greasy hair and cunning. He's sweet looking. Clean, cute as all get-out, and giving me a wide, blue-eyed stare framed with extraordinarily long black eyelashes. In short, he's a fresh-faced kid. But in that split second, I also see something else in his gaze. He knows what he's doing. He knows he's sweet. And he's daring me. This completely throws me. We stare for a beat or two, sizing each other up. At this point, I should probably mention that I am in my early thirties, and I'm thinking this situation has *The Graduate* written all over it. But he had asked me a question, asked me if I liked it. Jeez. The gall of this kid is impressive, I'm impressed.

"I hardly think it's appropriate bus behaviour," I say to him.

He takes his hand away and waves it at the rest of the bus.

"What's appropriate bus behaviour? Boring?"

I look around. The usual sullen faces. Frowns. Vacant bus stares. I shrug and give him a tiny smile, bestow a maternal pat on his hand that now lies in his own lap, and turn back to the window, close my eyes again. Zip! The finger's back. My eyes fly open but I don't look down. Now he knows that I know that he knows what he's doing. Up the finger goes again, softly, lightly, small circling motions. It gets to the hem of my dress. I do nothing. I'm wondering what he's going to do, how far he'll go. We're playing chicken, for sure. But is that all we're playing, I wonder?

It never occurs to me that this could be a highly illegal activity. Instead, I can't help thinking about the kid himself. His audacity. I wonder what kind of man he will grow into. Will he be a Don Juan, a confident gigolo, a supremely gifted and sought after ladies' man? Or will he end up in the news, a headline, perpetrator of sexual assaults, murder? Will he need therapy? Does he need it now? Basically, I guess I'm wondering if he's fatally disturbed or just terminally arrogant. A highly charged libido is one thing—criminally charged, is something else entirely.

I am aware the hem of my dress now looms like some kind of turning point, a crossroads. I am consumed with its presence. The hem is burning a slash across my leg, white hot. His finger creeps under the hem a bit and retreats, cautiously roving back and forth along the border. I know he is waiting for a sign. And I can't help myself, I start to enjoy it. To my surprise, I am actually getting turned on by this . . . this boy. My breath is coming quicker, my heart speeding up, and unbelievably my panties are getting damp. I know for sure now that if I open my legs a fraction, part my thighs even so much as an inch, I am giving him permission. I am crazy, *this* is crazy. We're on a goddamn bus, for chrissake. There are people all around us now. Boring people, to be sure, but people all the same. And who's the grown-up here? Hmmm, guess that would be me, Yer Honour. This kid's balls are definitely in my court.

Yet . . . I imagine his hand moving inwards all the same, I imagine feeling his finger gently pressuring the crotch of my panties and slipping easily under the elastic. Who would it really hurt? I know he's probably got a raging hard-on right now, but there's no way I can look over. I would completely lose it. And still, his insistent finger cruises my hemline. So I go for it, thinking, what the hell. No, correction: I think what the hell am I doing?

I have heard it said that everyone has rape fantasies. Like my soldier dream, in some form or another. It's something about power, about loss of control, giving it up. When I was an adolescent, I used to fantasize about this boy in school. I knew he took a shortcut through the bushes behind the gas station on his way home every day. None of us was allowed to cut through the bushes, and most of us never did. But Teddy was stupid. That was what made him so attractive. He had flunked a couple years and was in my grade, but older. I used to lie in bed at night and think about going into the bushes and faking an injury. A sprained ankle or something. And I would just be lying there, passed out, looking all vulnerable and beautiful, and Teddy would find me on his way home from school. He would have to pick me up and carry me home. I even fantasized about pretending I had been attacked and raped. I would be crawling along the dirt, all scratched up and crying. And when Teddy found me, I would hold onto him real tight, and he would feel all protective and kiss the tears off my face, and carry me home. But I never did it.

All my friends say they have entertained a rape fantasy of some description, at some point in their lives. The scenarios always involve a struggle, a contest of wills or physical assertiveness, in which the victim inevitably and willingly succumbs. It's sexy in a dangerous sort of way. Traditionally, my female friends are the swooning victims in these fantasies and my male friends play the dominant role. True to my gender, I am always the target in my own fantasies, some of which extend into the realm of the extremely bizarre. The rapists can range from cloven-hooved devil creatures, smelling of sulphur, with horns and leathery snouts, to straight-laced Wall Street tycoons in impeccably tailored suits, or even nerdy scientists in starched lab coats holding clipboards. Of course, we all know the real thing would suck.

But here I am on the #9 Broadway with some teenager's finger brazenly finding its way up my leg and I am doing nothing to stop it. This is sexy and dangerous, after all. I part my thighs almost imperceptibly, feel them unstick, all dampness and heat and sweat. His hand breaches the hem. Now there are two fingers, index and middle, and they begin baby-stepping their way inward, tentative, towards my inner right thigh. I feel my dress slip over his hand and he keeps going, cautious but determined. I forget the other passengers. I am only aware of his presence, his young smell, the rhythm and heat of his breath, and his fingers boldly travelling my skin. We are testing each other, our roles in this transitory drama. I have no idea if I can keep it up, keep it going.

"Do you do this often?" I say now, just to say something.

His hand stops moving.

"What do you mean?" he whispers.

"I mean, is this what you do, just ride the bus all day long seeing what you can get away with?"

I give him a sideways glance and see two things. The straining crotch of his baggy shorts, and a little-boy look in his eyes that almost resembles hurt.

"No, just you," he says.

His fingers start up again, and I almost believe him.

THE DRIVER'S SEAT

INTERVIEW WITH BOB SMITH

Grant Buday

I met Bob Smith one afternoon in late August at the Grand Garage Bar & Grill in the Atrium Inn on East Hastings for beer and burger hour. At the next table sat some longshoremen talking about a worker who got hit by a crane hook. Solitary drinkers watching the TVs occupied the other tables. Smith is 54, an amiable guy with short fair hair and a moustache. He rides a motorcycle, and arrived wearing shorts and a black leather jacket. He's been driving a bus for eighteen years, though has degrees in Social Work and Engineering.

The first thing I do is clear up a rumour—the source of which I don't recall—by asking whether or not it's true that bus drivers are all armed.

This drops Smith into a serious expression, which brings out his resemblance to George C. Scott.

"Not that I know of."

Do you drive armed?

No. But there's two sides to the story. About a week ago a driver was assaulted by two guys. And what's interesting is the scuttlebutt that went around the bullpen.

Bullpen?

That's the room in the main station where the drivers get ready. A lot of people commiserated and talked about escalating violence and how the company has to step up its efforts to protect drivers. Yet a different group of drivers said, well, the guy who got it just didn't have the right stuff. You know, like from the Tom Wolfe book. The right stuff.

What do you think about that?

I think it's more a matter of luck. I mean, there's a plague on both their houses, the people who say it'll never happen to me because I've got the right stuff, and the people who want this safety net, a wire cage to separate you from the public.

Have you ever been assaulted?

No. I've never come close to an assault. I have a big mouth and can usually talk my way out of things. I mean, I have, in moments of rage, got out of my seat and gone back there to get the last word on somebody, and then said to myself even as I'm speaking: What am I doing? How could I forget that this guy got on with four friends?

Can you describe the good things about driving a bus?

One of the good things about being a driver is that you don't have to clean up any messes.

You mean the vomit and other delicacies left by passengers.

That's the job of the supervisors. I'll tell you a story. It's not my story. It belongs to a woman named Virginia. But it's my favourite bus story. She was on her way to the Kootenay Loop when an old man fell out of his seat and his false teeth rolled down the aisle and came to a rest at the base of the change box. She said to him, "Don't move." When the other passengers got out at the Loop, Virginia took a Kleenex, picked up the false teeth, left the bus and crossed to the supervisor and dropped them into his hand. "The rest," she said, "is in the bus."

Is that the best thing about driving?

One of them. When I first started—eighteen years ago—I was very happy. It was a great job. I'd been doing social work. Very stressful. The first two years of driving felt very free. No one was looking over my shoulder. I could interact—or not—with the passengers as I pleased. It was up to me.

And the next sixteen years?

Well, after a while I noticed I was running out of different ways of moving people to the back. I was repeating lines I knew I had used on the Broadway line, but never on the Tsawwassen line. I'd discovered too many congenial passengers who turned into intolerable racists or sexists after a block, and I started to avoid conversations rather than start them. But when the fun stops with the passengers—the real zinger about driving bus is that it's just you, the road, and your problems. That's the issue. You stare out that front window and stew. So you're always confronted with yourself. It's a mental loop.

Soon the longshoremen at the next table leave and are replaced by a group of young guys fresh from the PNE who drink only Coca-Cola. The waitress arrives with another round of beer for us and spots the tape recorder on the table. She leans toward it. "Hello."

I was wondering if there are drivers who love buses. You know, like people who love trains?

Oh yes. Definitely. There are bus nuts among both passengers and drivers. *Oh, I've never been on this one before!* There are even bus driver groupies. There's a former driver living in California who owns eighty buses.

Eighty buses?

All different models.

That's kind of crazy.

Yup.

But I get the sense that it's a job that could make you crazy. It would make me crazy, because I hate driving. So I wonder, is there a lot of drug use among drivers?

I don't know. I couldn't comment on that. Though there was one guy who smoked a lot and I said, you must drive stoned. What percentage of the last year have you driven stoned? And he said, Oh, eighty percent?

But not you.

No. I think it would just double the length of the shift.

Do you have any principles of the road?

Let me answer that this way. About a year ago they brought in a law wherein cars have to give way to buses. They have to.

It's the law.

Yes, it's now the law. Well, my driving hasn't changed a bit. I've got seventy-five people aboard, a schedule to keep, and I'm a lot bigger. You can wait eight-tenths of a second.

And the drivers who refuse to wait eight-tenths of a second?

That leads to my third, no, my second favourite bus driving story. I was turning left onto Lougheed from Willingdon. And this guy didn't want to let me in. So I made him let me in. I made him. And this is a three-light wait. So there he is behind me now—I can see him in my rearview, and he gets out of his car and comes up to my side window and he's in a rage. He's clawing at the window and yelling at me to open it up. Now, I ask you, why would I want to go and do that? So I turned to the passengers in the bus and said, Let's all point at this guy and laugh. And they did! We all pointed at him and laughed.

What did he do?

He got back in his car.

We laugh.

He was a very stupid man. He may have been of average intelligence before that, but there was no blood flowing to his brain at that moment. I must say it was a lovely moment.

What about those people who sit up there in the first seat and talk to the drivers?

I try to ignore them. They're usually crazy or fascist or both.

So you become hardened.

You have to. Or they crush your spirit. The trouble is that after awhile you begin to suspect the worst about people. It's hard not to see the state of the world, and the collapse of the political process, as a downhill slide, and blame people. All people. And that includes the people on the bus. Look, I drive on the North Shore. I spend the mornings taking Filipino nannies up the hill. Pick up the white trash that hire them, and then during the day pick up the same nannies who now have five kids in tow. It's slave labour, and there's nothing I can do about it.

How much do you make?

About twenty an hour.

Do you like driving in and of itself?

No.

What do you think draws others to the job?

There's a lot of drivers who wish they were cops. They like the uniform, the perceived authority, the intercom, and they want to control things. Like kids skateboarding. "You better not skateboard in the bus area. It's a non-skateboarding area!"

Laughter.

It just seems to me they're making work for themselves.

There's the automatic assumption that the bus driver is responsible for maintaining civility amongst passengers.

Just last week there was a situation where there were six teenage boys on the bus. At the back as usual. And two girls. But they were separate parties. And this fellow comes up to me at one point and insists I kick those guys off the bus. A very insistent guy. I said why. He said they were swearing at the girls and calling them names. Well I looked and it seemed to me that the girls were fine. I said if I do that everyone's going to miss their connection for the SeaBus. So I didn't do anything. The guy says no one should have to put up with this. I say, Listen, I operate under a principle, and it's this: Everybody, eventually, gets off. That went over like water off a duck's back. He didn't even hear it. What does he do? He goes back to his seat—which was two seats away from the assholes in question.

So there's a definite potential for violence.

In eighteen years of driving I know of only one guy who's been killed, a passenger, and it was because the poor bastard was smoking on the bus.

He got killed for smoking on the bus?

Now this driver was an ex member of the Ku Klux Klan who had become a survivalist. And nobody was ever going to sass him. These guys get on, drunk, and go to the back and light up smokes. He tells them to get off. They come up and demand transfers since they have to get off. They were being belligerent, putting their faces too close to his and everything. So the driver sticks an eight-inch blade into one of them and twists it in a circle the way he'd been taught in his military training and the guy's guts spill out.

What happened to the driver?

He got off the charge. They didn't let him drive a bus again. He went into maintenance.

Maintenance?

Maintenance.

Where is he now?

Gone.

What's the most common cause of conflict?

Fare disputes are probably the main reason for fisticuffs. Here's a story I heard in the cafeteria at Oakridge, oh, ten years ago with some other drivers. We were sitting around talking and of course the stories come out. Now in this particular case a guy tried getting on with an expired transfer. The driver—one of these work-to-rule obsessives—said it was no good. The guy—drunk—reached into his pocket and came up with another transfer, but it was expired too. The driver tells him to get off. The drunk says since he has to get off he wants a new transfer. The driver refuses. So they eventually get into this amazing fight. And as the guy describes it he had the drunk down on the floor of the bus and he was giving it to him left and right and beating the shit out of the guy. Well, the driver finishes the story and sits back and waits for comments, but no one says a word. Finally I just sort of lean forward, you know, and I say, What if you'd have just given him the transfer? The guy says, Well, nothin' I guess. And all the other drivers there suddenly piped up and said, Yeah, I'd've just given him the transfer.

Lots of laughter.

I left feeling proud for some reason. Of the guys. It was beautiful, because the whole macho scene vanished. It was probably just lucky, but it's a favourite memory.

How about when people throw all kinds of nickels and pennies into the box to make a big clatter but you know they're short?

I have a line I use. I let them on and I give them their transfer, but I always say: You believe that's a reasonable down payment, do you?

What's the reaction?

They pretend not to hear. But I have the satisfaction of them knowing they're not fooling anyone. They know that I don't give a shit.

The talk veers into politics, unions, and then literature. Smith says he's been reading the American novelist David Foster Wallace on the irony of TV, though his favourite novelist is Don Delillo, author of the best book he's read in the last ten years, *Underworld*. It's a gorgeous snapshot of a boomer's life, he says. Mine.

I get the sense that politics is important to you.

We had so many opportunities that have been lost. The union movement has largely died here. I started driving bus for political reasons. We had a marvellous left caucus with its own newspaper that was respected and taking up the big questions of nationalism, sexism, racism and the rest. Nationalism won out, a Canadian union got the franchise, and the caucus split on how to deal with the new union. Bus drivers are not industrial unionists, per se. They're like the posties, the guys who walk the routes. They think of themselves as Lone Ranger types. They're out there, independent, independent from their brothers and sisters sorting mail inside. They're thinking: Don't mess with me because I got a good thing going. The trouble is, they don't realize they no longer have a good thing going. My paycheques are the same size as they were ten years ago, and the expenses have gone through the roof. It used to be a good paying job.

But they're pretty solid union jobs comparatively.

Yeah, right. Compared to what though? I once had a spat with a woman on my bus on a statutory holiday. It was one of those rare events when I got out of my seat because this woman objected to my glibness. I finished wagging my finger at her in the middle of the aisle of the bus and some guy said, "You should be happy because it's a holiday and you're making double-time." I said to him that it was an undeniable drawback of our civilization that you are either working or you're unemployed, and that neither option was particularly attractive. Two days later I get called in by my supervisor for a complaint hearing. We get paid an hour to hear these things. The woman phoned to say that a driver had said the whole problem of bus driving was you were carrying either immigrants or the unemployed. I got twenty bucks for coming in to explain my side of the story, but it still annoys me that she missed one of my better lines.

Have you ridden buses in other countries?

Oh yes. Mexico. I go to Mexico a lot. I love riding the buses in Mexico. The people are so courteous to each other. Veterans of wars, bus wars.

Yes, I've noticed that. On intercity buses people often offer a general buenos dias to everyone aboard and then say adios when they get off. You don't see that here. I often find it's a bold social gesture just to say thanks to the driver when I get off.

Keep trying. When I started driving bus, I was surprised by the number of people who said Thank you! Now I resent those who don't.

Thanks for talking to me.

ABOUT THE AUTHORS

TAMMY ARMSTRONG's work has appeared in numerous literary journals. Her first collection of poetry, *Bogman's Music*, won the Alfred G. Bailey Award from the New Brunswick Writers Federation last year and will be published by Anvil Press in Fall 2001. As she's never gotten around to learning how to drive, she endures that circus called public transit.

GREGORY BETTS' work has been published in *Geist* magazine and *The Windsor Review*. He is currently working at York University where the buses refuse to cross his picket line.

BONNIE BOWMAN is a Vancouver writer and editor whose debut novel, *Skin*, was published this year as the 1999 winner of the three-day novel contest sponsored by Anvil Press. Ms. Bowman has paid her dues on public transit over the years and survived to relate one incident. She is currently working on her second novel, *Strain*, which will feature twisted characters not unlike those found on a 3 A.M. downtown bus crawl in any given city.

GRANT BUDAY is the author of a collection of short stories, three novels, and a travel memoir entitled *Golden Goa*. His most recent novel, *White Lung*, was a finalist for the City of Vancouver book award.

TONY BURGESS is the author of *The Hellmouths of Bewdley*, *Pontypool Changes Everything* and *Casearea*. He lives in Wasaga Beach, Ontario.

EVE CORBEL's comix have been published in *Geist*, *Herizens*, *B.C. BeeScene*, and *Not My Small Diary*, among other publications.

MATT CRISCI is an award-winning newspaper reporter and author of *Observation of a Kind*™, a hardbound collection of human-interest short stories. He recently completed a first novel, *Fanny, I Love You,* based upon a true story, and is currently working on a screenplay of same. Classified as an expert on consumer motivation and behaviour, Mr. Crisci has been elected to *"Who's Who in American Business."*

CARLA ELM wrote her first poem at the age of five. Her recent writing has been published in the 1999 and 2000 issues of *Pearls*, an in-house anthology of Douglas College writing students. During summer 2000 she attended the B.C. Festival of the Arts in Nelson as an *otherwords* fiction writing delegate. Her novel-in-progress addresses nature and coincidences.

M.A.C. FARRANT is the author of six collections of satirical and humorous short fiction, most recently *Girls Around the House* (Polestar). Her work has been dramatized for television and radio, appears regularly in various magazines, including *Adbuster's* and *Geist* where she is a correspondent. She is the Co-Producer and Host of the popular Sidney Reading Series. She lives in Sidney, B.C. Canada.

TIM HEARSEY has put in his time behind the wheel of a cab to be able to remain behind the steel of a guitar. Currently working with other local artists as a writer/producer/engineer, he is also involved in a documentary film, in addition to performing with the Jim Byrnes Band.

JONATHAN HIMSWORTH has never been published before. Other than the odd bounced cheque, this is his first material anybody showed interest in. A defender of public transport, a supporter of world football, part-time radio DJ and telephone operator, he lives in Vancouver with a revolving procession of roommates.

MARK ANTHONY JARMAN, author of *19 Knives, New Orleans is Sinking*, and *Salvage King Ya!*, teaches at the University of New Brunswick and directs the Wired Writing Studio at the Banff Centre.

RYAN KNIGHTON's writing has appeared in numerous Canadian journals and magazines. His first book of poetry, *Swing in the Hollow*, is forthcoming from Anvil Press. He teaches in the English Dept. at Capilano College and edits *The Capilano Review*.

VIVIEN LOUGHEED is a freelance travel writer living in Prince George, B.C. She is the author of *Central America by Chickenbus, Kluane National Park Hiking Guide* and *Forbidden Mountains*, a story about her illegal journey across restricted areas of Tibet. Vivien is also the co-author of *Tungsten John*, a hiking adventure she shared with her partner, John Harris.

MARION LYDBROOKE's stories have been published in England and Canada. At six she wrote a story about a bus taking its passengers for free rides. She still believes all public transport should be free. She lives in Toronto.

JEAN MALLINSON's prose and poetry has appeared in a variety of literary periodicals and anthologies. Her collection of short stories, *I Will Bring You Berries*, was published by Caitlin Press in 1987; she is co-author of *Quintet*, a book of poetry published by Ekstasis Press in 1998.

BUD OSBORN is a poet and poverty-rights activist whose work has been published in numerous magazines and anthologies. He is the author of three books of poetry, *Lonesome Monsters, Hundred Block Rock,* and *Keys to Kingdoms* which was the recipient of the City of Vancouver Book Prize, 1999.

STEPHEN OSBORNE is the editor of *Geist* magazine, and author of *Ice & Fire: Dispatches from the New World*.

BRIAN PRATT is a poet and bus driver. He lives in Burnaby, B.C.

BOB SMITH is a retired industrial engineer, a retired social worker, a retired bookstore clerk, a retired steel worker, and a retired truck painter. He has been wanting to be a retired bus driver for the last 19 years.

BETSY TRUMPENER currently lives in BC's northern interior, where she works as a newspaper reporter. Her fiction and non-fiction writing has been published in *The Malahat*

Review, Event, This Magazine, NOW Magazine, the *Globe and Mail,* and broadcast on CBC Radio's *This Morning.*

HEATHER WATSON has used public transit on four continents and lived to write about it. Besides writing and travelling, she divides her time between PR work and playing with toys for money. Future projects include a solo musical comedy act and a documentary film to be shot in the UK.

That's it, folks! For now, at any rate. Putting together this anthology has been so much fun—we want to do it again ... though how soon is anybody's guess. It will all depend, of course, on the material—and that's where you come in. Got a good, true, public transit tale? Well, if you do, we encourage you to send it on in, and when we have enough great material, we'll issue *Exact Fare Only II*, another volume of wild, wacky, and humorous pubilc transit tales.

Send your tales of public transit to:
    True Tales of Public Transit
    Anvil Press Publishers
    175 East Broadway, Suite 204-A
    Vancouver, B.C.
    V5T 1W2
    CANADA